ELLE HARTFORD

Strong in Love
Pomegranate Cafe Romance #2

Phoenix & Kelpie

First published by Phoenix & Kelpie Press 2023

Copyright © 2023 by Elle Hartford

This novel is entirely a work of fiction. The names, characters and incidents portrayed in it are the work of the author's imagination. Any resemblance to actual persons, living or dead, events or localities is entirely coincidental.

First edition

ISBN: 979-8-9872017-7-0

This book was professionally typeset on Reedsy.
Find out more at reedsy.com

Contents

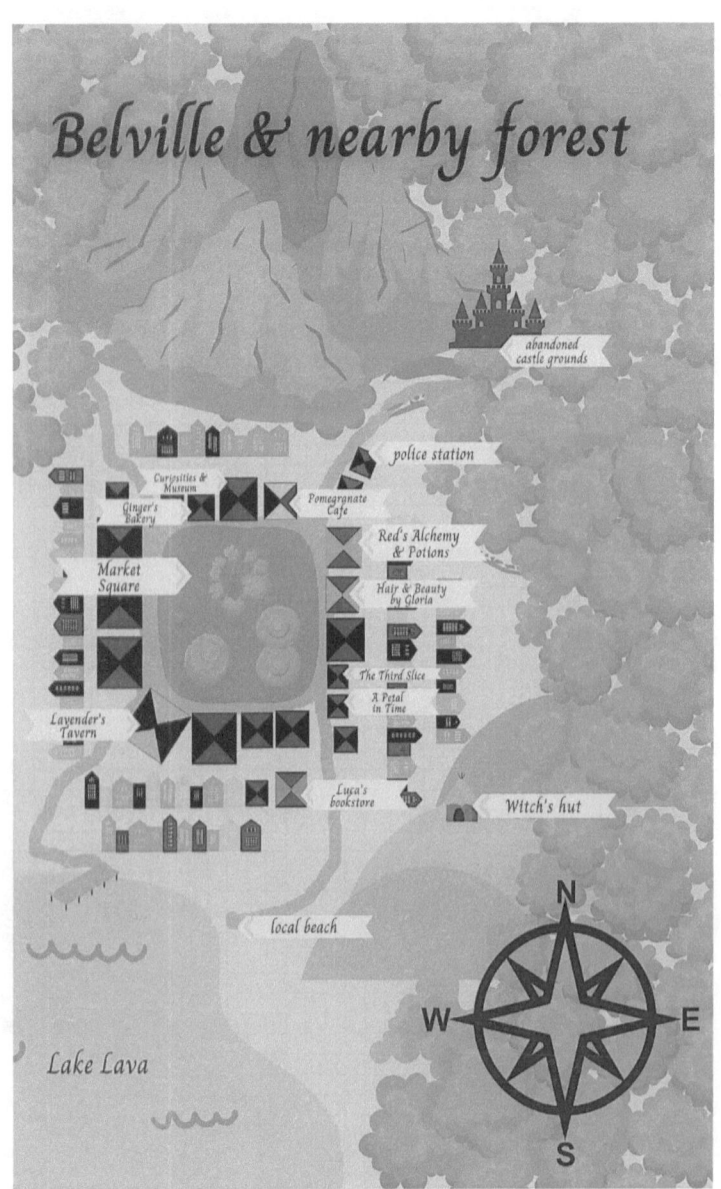

Belville & nearby forest

abandoned castle grounds

police station

Curiosities & Museum

Ginger's Bakery

Pomegranate Cafe

Red's Alchemy & Potions

Market Square

Hair & Beauty by Gloria

The Third Slice

A Petal in Time

Lavender's Tavern

Luca's bookstore

Witch's hut

local beach

N

W   E

S

Lake Lava

Prologue

Sakura

Well, it isn't every day you help a dragon, is it?

Not that I'm trying to brag, of course. But I think what strikes me most about this whole affair was how *unusual* it was. It was odd in the first place, really, not to think of Daisy and Sir Rowan in the same sentence. When I first arrived in Belville, before the Pomegranate Café was even a whisper in my mind, they were together. I suppose I'd simply assumed they would stay that way forever. There is something awfully timeless about dragons and knights, after all.

. . . But now I'm starting to ramble. Let me set the scene instead. It was summer in Belville, the Pomegranate Café's first summer, and nearly the summer solstice—you might also know it as Litha or Midsummer. I was determined to make Midsummer's Eve the biggest party the whole mountain had ever seen. This was a bit of a tall order, since rumor had it that on the previous Midsummer's Eve, Red the alchemist had solved a centuries-old cold case in the hapless local Witch's basement.

Some Witches simply have no luck.

I, of course, know better: I make my own luck. I started planning my party early, and all my plans were skeleton-free. The thing about Midsummer is that it's all about abundance and celebrating what's right in front of you, the simple, natural things. It's a beloved holiday of wild gods and of pixies—some people will tell you the *fairies* are the ones who love it, but that's patently untrue. "Pixies play on Midsummer's day," as the saying goes.

Now, I'm not much of one for pixies, myself. You'll hear all about them later on, from Daisy, and I'm sure you'll be able to guess why I usually avoid them. However I certainly wasn't going to ban them from their own holiday. I decided to build a café menu based on favorite midsummer foods like honey cakes and floral flavors, and that meant I needed one flower in particular: wild meadowsweet, which the pixies call Queen of the Meadow.

So, off I went to the florist, A Petal in Time. *Out of stock,* they tell me, as if Belville wasn't surrounded by a massive and plentiful forest! Well, I went to Red's alchemy shop at once, and to be honest I was glad to give *her* my business instead, because Red is a dear friend. She can always be counted on to have odd plants around. And what did Red tell me? *All* of the meadowsweet on the entire mountain was now under the protection of Daisy's pixies, who had apparently taken up an interest in gardening.

I never did see why gardening should get in the way of a good party.

Red offered to put me in touch with the pixies, of course,

because she's a dear and can't help but *help*. Her plan involved having me talk to Sugar, a rogue pixie who seems to haunt Red's kitchen. I knew right then that something was up, and I was right. That's where the real adventure began.

I'll tell you one more thing, because I know that our star-crossed lovers won't: when I moved into town nearly a year ago, *everyone* knew about Sir Rowan and Daisy. You might say they were a sort of power couple around town. One name went with the other—like pixies and midsummer, or romance and tea—and honestly, their love was the sort of thing that inspires stories. (In fact, Red *did* get the two of them to write their origin story, and you can find it in Belville's bookstore to this day, because Luca—that's our bookseller—is a determined romantic.)

Well, nice as it was, all of that ended as summer began. No one knows exactly what happened; if I had to bet, I'd imagine it has something to do with knightly honor gone too far—never could stand the stuff, myself.

Oh, but you don't want to listen to my speculation. What you really want is to hear the story from the romantic couple themselves!

One

Mistakes Made

Daisy

If I'm completely honest with you, I made a mistake.

I knew that, even then. But I couldn't figure out *what* the mistake had been.

I'm Daisy, by the way. You'd think that I'd have the hang of this by now! I suppose I am not a natural storyteller. You see, I am a guardian—I come from a family of them. My family has protected the mountain pixies from the town pixies down in Belville for a long time. There was a feud between different groups of pixies once, though it's mostly over now. None of the pixies on either side seem interested in causing trouble these days—or if they do, they don't let me see it, since I'm a dragon.

Naturally I don't go around town as a dragon, though. I

have a charm that helps me change into human form, which is helpful for talking to people and even for helping the pixies. I don't have much magic myself, especially when I'm human, but they—the pixies, I mean—have magic by the bucket full.

Maybe that's the problem, come to think of it. Because when you have a *little* magic, you inevitably want *more,* and then you start looking to control the future . . .

Anyway, I had meant to start telling you about the day I went to talk to Sakura at her charming café. That's probably not the right place to start the story—probably I should start by talking about how and why I broke things off with Sir Rowan. But I just can't talk about that yet.

And now that I say that, I realize that going to see a shadow witch about love was probably also a mistake.

But it was also a business meeting, of sorts. We sat in the back corner of Sakura's café with tea and lemon cakes and she was going on at considerable length about her plans for a magical party on Litha, the summer solstice . . .

"It'll be the biggest thing we've done since Valentine's Day. It'll go all night, and then we'll watch the sunrise together. Witches often use meadowsweet in divination, you know, so I was thinking we'd set out little 'see your future' kits with a sprig of the flower and a white candle at each table, inside and out on the patio—if you agree, of course. Just for fun. People can burn the flowers and see what images pop up in the flames. I'll have lots of fire protection spells up, of course. That'd keep everyone occupied at the beginning of the night, and then we can tell stories afterward, like in previous Midsummer celebrations. Plus we'll have flower teas, and Glacial's already baking up all kinds of special treats. And Ryuko and Dusty have *promised* that by then, the second floor will be open, so I'm thinking we could do a shower of flower petals from the balcony! What do you think?"

Sakura finished talking, briefly, with her pale face flushed and blue eyes bright. Even though she deals in shadow magic, everything about her is bright, and rounded, and soft, and she always made me feel rather gangly and awkward even though I liked her immediately. White hair cut smooth and short framed her face, though she has never struck me as old. Her bright pink Pomegranate Café apron layered over a fluttery white dress and animated movements added to her energetic air. I looked up, following the gesture of her hands, and nearly hit my head on a shelf tucked just above a miniature moon lamp.

"I always forget about people being tall," Sakura clucked sympathetically. At just barely five feet, she fit into the little tea nook perfectly. "I always pick this table back here for quiet conversations, and forget about that shelf! I can't tell you how many times Ryu has hit his head, exactly like you did. Maybe we'll have to move it. I'll add it to the list for later. They only do work on the building after we've closed for the day, of course."

"Of course," I agreed, my head swimming. It wasn't because of the bump. Until about a year ago, I lived entirely alone—well, alone with my pixies—in a cave on the mountain. Carpenters and tea rooms and quiet conversations still gave me feelings of nausea sometimes.

Especially without Rhys—or rather, Sir Rowan—nearby.

I tried to clear the thought from my head, but I think Sakura saw it. Can shadow witches do that—read thoughts? I'm not sure, but I've always had a suspicion that Sakura can. Sometimes I think she seems like a pixie, but then she does something completely unexpected and catches me off guard.

"That's enough about me and my plans for now," she decided,

giving me an unsettlingly perceptive look. "We can iron out the details of the flowers and the party later. Call me silly, Daisy, but I get the feeling there's something else you wanted to discuss."

"Well, I . . ."

"When I asked Red about taking you a message and she told me to talk to *Sugar*, of all people, I knew something was up. I figured she'd tell me to talk to Sir Rowan, since he works for her and all. And in his spare time, isn't he supposed to be the go-between for the pixies and the town?"

"Well, yes, technically, but that's just old superstition really, especially now that the different groups of pixies get along alright. He should be free to—"

"But I let it go at first," Sakura continued blithely. "Until now. I had expected to deal with you via messenger, be it Sugar or knight. And yet here you are, in person. I can count the number of times I've seen you in person on one hand, Daisy."

"Yes, well, I'm trying to get better," I mumbled.

"Oh, don't go to any trouble on my account. There's nothing wrong with being a recluse, especially considering you *do* have a very important duty, up there on the mountain." Sakura gave me another searching look and I shrunk into my shoulders, trying to hide. "I'm only thinking that, since you *are* here in person when we could just as easily have traded messages about the meadowsweet, you must want something from me."

"I—want something?" I sounded more like a mouse than a dragon, I know. It was the truth of it that startled me. I hadn't expected townsfolk to be so involved in my affairs!

Another mistake.

"Yes, and I'm more than happy to oblige, believe me." Sakura settled her elbows on the table and her round chin in her hands, smiling brightly. "So what is it? Would you like to talk something over? Something to do with Sir Rowan, perhaps?"

"No," I said. Probably too quickly. Sakura's white eyebrows rose, and before she could ask anything, I hurried on. "It's just that—well, the pixies have been telling me—I've been—lonely," I said at last, only barely avoiding the word that the pixies had actually used, which was *mopey*. "I know with your café you see all kinds of people, and R—well—I've heard you're very good about relationships. So I was thinking, maybe, you might . . . That is, would you—do you think you could—set me up on a date?"

Two

Work and Worms

Rhys

I am not accustomed to telling stories in this manner. Normally I keep careful notes in my journal, and, if curiosity strikes later, I refer to those notes to recount past events.

However, I must admit that the notes in my journal from the time period in question are very scant.

Would that my memory was less vivid . . .

Nonetheless, I remember very clearly watching Daisy enter the Pomegranate Café. I did not wish to. I was not *trying* to observe the way her yellow summer dress outlined the grace of her figure or the glint of her red hair in the afternoon sun. But as I was stocking the front windows of Red's Alchemy & Potions, I had no choice but to notice Miss Sakura's latest customer.

Especially one as beautiful as my lady.

But she *wasn't* my lady, not any more. For days, I'd attempted to remind myself of that fact. I'd even written it on a napkin in the tavern—I couldn't bring myself to actually write the facts of the matter in my journal, which was languishing in my old room upstairs. All the reminders failed to make my new world feel any less surreal. So, I must admit, I'd finally lapsed into a kind of dreamlike denial. There was a certain reason to it: I couldn't accept reality, so therefore I would dwell in a realm that was half memory, half wish. It is not as uncommon as one might hope.

Unfortunately, it had been nearly a full moon of living this way, and the people around me were beginning to notice.

"Here, I just finished the last batch of fertilizers. I thought the colored bottles would look good in the window with the gardening display—but let's put them somewhere they won't get *too* much direct sun, otherwise who knows what kinds of bacteria we'll be growing . . . Sir Rowan?"

"Hmm," I replied.

Miss Red, my employer and the alchemist alluded to in her shop's name, went on to say something which various witnesses have since informed me was along the lines of, "Because the last thing we need is a repeat of that worm affair that took over Sakura's café, right?"

I continue to insist that what I *heard* was . . . well, something to do with the café. And perhaps the word "fair." It's just possible that I wasn't actually listening. Miss Daisy had disappeared into the café, and suddenly I was very thirsty. So, I assumed Miss Red meant to ask me to fetch tea or some other sundry café beverage; accordingly I stood and said, "Good idea."

When Miss Red failed to get out of my way, and in fact continued to stare at me with an unbecoming scrunched-up look on her otherwise astute face, I began—very slowly—to realize something was wrong.

"Worms?" she asked, a flush rising behind her light brown skin. She set one gloved hand on her hip. "Worms are a good idea?"

I cleared my throat. "I don't recall worms entering the conversation."

"I don't think *you* were having a conversation," Miss Red retorted. I have found it is nearly impossible to argue with her in her own shop. The gloves, combined with some brightly-colored lab coat and a pair of goggles pushed up over her forehead, are her constant uniform, and they are clear evidence of her authority. In fact, everything about Miss Red is practicality itself: black hair pulled into a ponytail, a level, mellow voice, clear hazel eyes prone to scrutiny. She has always been a bit too smart for her own good.

"I merely supposed, miss, that you wanted something from the café—"

"I think I'd prefer a finished window display," my employer said dryly. I followed her gaze and saw that the specialty flower pots I'd been stacking were only half set, more a jumbled heap than a tidy pyramid. Likewise, the preserved blooms I'd intended to arrange into an eye-catching bouquet were scattered all across the floor of the bay window.

The disconcerting fact I have noticed about living in a dream-like state is that *time* becomes very slippery. Though I'll admit it took me longer than usual to think through new circumstances, apparently it had taken me much *less* time than usual to react. Looking at the mess in Miss Red's window, the only conclusion possible was that I'd stood too fast and knocked everything over.

And where, I couldn't help but wonder, *is my lady now?*

She might have already had her tea and left the café by now.

"Go easy on him, Red," a voice came from the back of the shop, where the sales counter stood. *Barked* is the appropriate word, both for the speaker and the tone. William, Red's companion and arcane familiar, appears to most as a rather large, rather shaggy black dog. Despite this he has considerable magic of his own, and has always had the kindness to look after me as a fellow magic-user in an otherwise very scientific shop. I do not often need such looking after, but I will admit that in that moment I was very grateful for it.

Of course, alarm eclipsed my gratitude as William then added, "He's got a lot on his mind, since he and Daisy broke up."

I will note here that arcane familiars, being magical beings created by sorcerers who themselves often eschew society, are not known for their tact.

The skepticism written across Miss Red's face was now replaced with concern. "You and Daisy *what?* How is that even possible? When? I'm so sorry, Sir Rowan!"

She immediately set her box of fertilizers to one side and took my arm, leading me to the back of the shop. At that point, I'd been working for Miss Red for more than a year, and had had ample time to observe her and William. In that detached, dreamlike way, I knew exactly what they would do: shepherd me into the overstuffed chairs in the tea corner, usually reserved for customers waiting for special orders, and there ply me with whatever experimental tea Miss Red had concocted that morning, and speak over each other in their efforts to be helpful and kind. They would eventually get the story from me; of that I was quite certain, and there was a sort of relief in that certainty. I have been alive for centuries, and yet I have not ever come across such insistent—and inquisitive—coworkers. But I have always wondered if perhaps I needed them.

Still, it must be said; as grateful as I was for William's concern and Miss Red's curiosity, my inner dream world was awash with longing to be called by my personal name, one I had only ever given to my lady.

Three

Wish List

Daisy

"Alright," said Sakura, as she poured herself another cup of creamy earl grey tea. "I might be able to help you, Daisy. Let's get an idea of what you're looking for first. Do you have any hard 'no's? You know, things that you *wouldn't* want in a potential date. Aside from the usual obvious red flags, of course."

"No knights," I said promptly. I did my best to hide my wince behind my own teacup, but it was empty, and I think the shadow witch noticed . . .

. . . But she was good enough not to mention it. "That's doable, seeing as there's only one in town that I know of." She *did* slide me a look then, but I ignored it, doing my best not to fidget in my seat. Or blush. Humans really are so vulnerable to this sort of thing!

After what seemed like an age, Sakura finally went on. "So what are some things you *would* like in a date? You know, personality, values, that kind of thing."

The question scared me at first. I actually hadn't thought that much about all this. I didn't want to admit that to Sakura, though. The last thing I needed was another lecture from a well-meaning bystander. I'd been getting nothing but unsolicited advice from the pixies for weeks.

I tried sipping at my tea to stall for time, but, of course, it was empty. Without a word, Sakura reached out to fill it for me. That gave me an idea.

"I'd like someone kind," I said, all in a rush, as if I was afraid it'd hurt.

Sakura nodded as she pushed milk and honey in my direction. "What else?"

"Thoughtful," I added. But then, not wanting to seem like I was just describing *her*, I hastened to add a few more things. "And respectful, of course. Of me *and* the pixies, I mean."

"That's a given," Sakura agreed.

"And—well—I am very old, myself—you might have known that. Or guessed it. So, it'd be good to find someone who . . ."

". . . has a similarly long lifespan?" Sakura asked.

I wondered if she was making fun of me—I'm well aware that most humans consider dragons to be very strange, or even almost divine. I wondered if perhaps it struck her as funny, that I should hope for someone at least somewhat similar to me, especially in such a tiny alpine town. (Not that I could ever bear going all the way to a city—could you *imagine*?) But for as close as I looked at her face, I couldn't see any trace of amusement. Eventually, I nodded. "Or, at least, someone who doesn't mind if I'm—well—a bit ancient, really. And obviously very devoted to my—duty." It seemed strange to call guarding the pixies *work.*

"You mentioned that part already," Sakura reminded me. She wasn't unkind—she had the sort of practical attitude I'd often noticed in Lavender, the local innkeeper, when discussing business. "So far, we have kind, thoughtful, respectful, and preferably old. Or ageless. Anything else?"

"Er . . . Obviously they'd have to be okay with, well, *me . . .*"

"Daisy." Sakura reached out and put her hand over mine, which without thinking I'd clasped nervously around my necklace. "Sweetie, you're just describing the bare minimum here. I'm *definitely* not going to set you up with some jerk who'd have a problem with you being who you are, or with the pixies, for that matter."

I pulled my hands away—not because I don't like Sakura, of course, it's just that I'm really not that used to being touched. And I was frustrated. I knew she was right, but I didn't know what else to ask for. It all felt too *big.* "Well—but the pixies *can* be awfully trying . . . even for someone who's usually very patient and steady . . ."

"How about this," Sakura said, leaning back and considering me in a way that felt almost maternal. "Picture yourself on vacation. Not a pixie in sight. Don't worry, they're all being cared for! But in the meantime, you're out by yourself, and you're having an adventure. So: what kind of person would you like to meet on your travels? Who would make this the most fun?"

Rhys, I thought.

But that was wrong. *Anyone* but *him,* I reminded myself.

We've already been there. I took a deep breath and tried to really picture what Sakura had said. Who would I like to meet? "Someone . . . someone with a sense of humor. Who could make the time pass by, but also make it feel like we have forever together. Someone to sit with quietly, but also someone not afraid of racing or flying if we want to. Someone strong enough to see that sometimes I need help, and to let me help them, too. Someone I can be free with."

I opened my eyes—I hadn't even realized I'd closed them. Sakura was smiling at me.

"Now that's a better list," she said. "And remember—this is one date, that's all, so try not to put too much pressure on it. Just think of it as fun. Think of it as wasting time."

Wasting time? That seemed a little strange. I wondered what she meant by it . . .

But Sakura had already moved on. "Is there anything else you'd like to add?"

"No, I—I think that's everything." I was proud of myself for having come up with it all.

"Alright, that just leaves one small detail," said the shadow witch, delicately sipping her tea.

"What is it?" I asked, moving to finally sip some of my tea as well.

"You do realize that everything you've just said perfectly describes Sir Rowan, right?"

I spat my tea out. It was bitter—I'd forgotten to actually add the milk or honey Sakura had passed to me.

"Well," she added thoughtfully, "everything *except* the part about not being a knight."

14

Four

Tea and Sympathy

Rhys

"So what happened? You're going to have to tell us eventually, Sir Rowan. You know how things are around here."

"Don't bother him, Red! He'll say something when he's ready!"

"And when will that be, once he's knocked over a shelving unit full of glass and potions? Or stumbled into the kiln? No offense, Sir Rowan. But you've said it yourself, we have to keep a tight ship around here. And you've never been above prompting me to talk when there's something on *my* mind . . ."

"Like you ever have anything as important as losing your true love on your mind."

"Hey, don't be rude! If that's how you feel about it, William, then you should be helping me talk to him."

The bell above the shop door interrupted this dialogue which, I must admit, I was becoming rather used to. There was a lullaby-like quality to the consistency of Miss Red and William's bickering.

"I'm sorry, we're going to have to take a quick bre—oh, it's you, Luca," Miss Red said as she turned toward the sound of the bell.

A tall, slim figure in floor-length black robes entered: Belville's official scholar, Luca. Like scholars elsewhere, he ran the town's one bookstore and often assisted with queries regarding local history, and even in the summer heat refused to part with his 'uniform.' I could relate to this habit of propriety, but little else. Luca was, as usual, almost impossibly cheerful. "Hi, Red! Hi everyone! I was just heading to the café for an afternoon snack and I thought—what's wrong with Sir Rowan?"

I suppose that when Mister Luca mentioned the café, I might have groaned. Audibly. Not at all something I would normally do, I assure you. But it was a very unusual afternoon.

"Heartbreak," said William, rather unhelpfully. "He needs *space*."

"What he *needs* is to talk to his friends," Miss Red argued. "Luca, why don't you join us, if you can. Flip over our 'closed' sign first though, will you? We might take you up on that offer of snacks from the café . . . in a minute."

Never has *in a minute* sounded so ominous.

The shop was unnaturally quiet as Mister Luca obeyed Miss Red's requests. I had observed in the past that whenever Mister Luca was visiting, there was very rarely silence. Like many other scholars, he has that tendency to narrate his current thoughts aloud, or to explain a simple decision with a long anecdote, usually beginning with "when I got up this morning" or "so I've been thinking, for a while now…". I am not, strictly speaking, enamored of such behavior.

But with that said—I *do* have the utmost respect for Mister Luca. I happen to know that he is far older and far wiser than his habitual manner suggests. And it goes without saying that I couldn't respect Miss Red more than I already do; for her years, she has done and learned much; I would never work for her if that was not the case. William, naturally, demands his own kind of respect as a magical creature.

I found myself forced to sit in a chair, looking up at the three of them around me. For an instant I had the most uncanny feeling of waking up. And for just a very brief moment, I confess I was terrified.

"Miss Red, I appreciate your concern," I attempted to say, though even *I* could hear how strangled my own voice sounded, "but really, I must protest. There is no need for all of this."

"Sir Rowan." It was Mister Luca who spoke, his cheerfulness having faded into gentle sympathy. His dark skin and clothing drew attention to his green eyes, which shone at me earnestly. "What can we do for you?"

Bring my lady back.

Next thing I knew, my cheeks were damp, my head in my hands, my hands on my knees. My skin, pale at the best of times, had become clammy; the hair I kept combed back from my face was mussed, dark strands falling into my eyes. My companions were too kind to comment, however. William was sitting beside me, the fur of his shaggy coat pressing into my trousers. Miss Red had seated herself on the floor on my other side, leaning against the edge of my chair as she passed out steaming cups. Mister Luca was sitting in the other armchair, leaning forward, looking at me with such intensity that for a moment I could see exactly what he and Miss Red had found in one another.

"I'm so sorry," Mister Luca was saying. "I should have known better than to ask."

I tried to protest, but Miss Red interrupted firmly, pressing a cup into my hands. "Don't apologize, Luca, Sir Rowan. Either of you. Contrary to what William may say, we've all been there. And what we can do right now is listen."

"But he might not want to talk," William rumbled.

Grateful once more, I placed my free hand onto William's wide head. Both he and his mistress were right. I cleared my throat. "I—I did not intend to let anyone know."

"We noticed," Miss Red replied. I could not see her face as she looked down at her tea, but I knew she was displeased. And—for the first time—I could see why she might be. After all, I *had* often sought to give her advice. For me to deny her the same opportunity . . .

. . . Well, wasn't that exactly what my lady had accused me of?

I sighed. "It happened three weeks and six days ago. I thought—I don't know. I thought it wouldn't matter to anyone in town. I will, of course, continue to perform all my duties, both here and as a messenger for the pixies. I did not want to trouble you with it."

As I mentioned previously, I do have some small magic of my own. Often I use it to heighten my own perception. One thing you learn as a knight—and again as a disgraced knight—is that observation is the best defense one could hope for. But in that moment I needed neither magic nor honed observational skills to recognize that my words had an effect. Miss Red said nothing, but she might as well have been seething. William was leaning into my leg so forcefully that, had I been standing, I am certain I would have fallen over.

It was Mister Luca who spoke. "It isn't any trouble, Sir Rowan, and I really don't think Red is worried about your efficiency. We're worried about *you*. We *want* to know, so that we can help. Do you—do you want to tell us why it happened, maybe?"

For a moment, I endeavored to collect my thoughts. The reality I'd been avoiding was crashing over me. I finally broke, speaking in an uncontrolled whisper. "My lady wished not to *hold me back*. That is how she said it. I had known for some time that something was on her mind, of course, and that she had been distant at times, and of course with the change in the seasons the pixies have been particularly active and weighing on her mind, but she made some allusion to a story, and I didn't understand it, it might have been something those cursed pixies told her I suppose, although I thought we were quite decided on that already, and we've certainly had enough time to go over it, and there's no reason it should come up now, but nevertheless my lady has been troubled ever since Ostara, and somehow I could never figure out *why*, and I could never make it go *away*, and—"

The sentence had no end; it simply died in my throat, as I'd run out of breath. *Gods help me if I ever think to make light of Mister Luca's run-on thoughts again,* I thought, and might have even laughed aloud at myself if I had had the energy.

"To hold you back," Mister Luca repeated thoughtfully, swirling his tea. "I wonder why she thought she would?"

"What do you mean, you'd decided something already?" Miss Red asked without looking up.

My own gaze drifted vaguely over the books and potion bottles beyond. "The pixies my lady is Guardian of have a very specific mythology. Thousands of years ago, they were persecuted by the pixies who live here in town; this is why they live in hiding high on the mountain. One of their deities granted them their home on Belville Mountain, and also gifted them the egg that would become Daisy's family line. And as it turns out . . . we discovered last winter that that deity was, in fact, my mother. And as such, the pixies believe I—I have a role to play in their mythology too—as a guide, of sorts, for their re-emergence in society."

William stirred. "Your *mother?*"

I said nothing. With deities, I have found, one must tread very carefully.

"Fascinating," said Mister Luca—a scholar and bookseller to his very core. "I *have* to get that all on paper one day. Maybe we can arrange an interview with both groups of pixies—once all this is settled, of course," he added with a guilty look at Miss Red.

"So theoretically you would be working *with* Daisy," Miss Red said in her turn. "But apparently she thought—what? That the role was too confining for you?"

"She mentioned that the pixies have a tendency to turn everything into a momentous affair—a romanticized, melodramatic, unrealistic expectation. I myself have seen that," I confessed. Hearing the three of them discuss the matter aloud made it so much easier to speak freely. "For example, what they view as gifts from a deity could also be interpreted as . . . well, to put it bluntly, goods that were taken from somewhere else and created a great deal more trouble in the long run."

"Stolen goods?" William summarized. "Are we still talking

about your mother here?"

I grimaced. "A beloved minor deity of the forest . . . who, like many natural deities, believes in taking a rather circuitous and *unconventional* approach to fate."

"Well, everyone has unexpected sides to them," Miss Red observed neutrally.

"And that's Daisy's problem, isn't it? She worried that she, like the pixies, was putting unfair expectations on you," Mister Luca mused. He looked up and, seeing myself and the others staring at him, flushed. "Well, I don't know that—but of course it makes sense. Don't you think?"

I wondered. Mister Luca has always been the more intuitive, between himself and Miss Red. Perhaps it was some kind of fate that brought him to the potions shop that afternoon, to share his valuable insight.

"And when she said that—or something like it—what did you say? How do *you* feel about it, Sir Rowan?" asked Miss Red.

"I feel that fairness and expectations, while reasonable considerations in their own right, have no bearing on the fact that my heart has been hers from the moment I first saw her. Nothing—no new role, no mythological revelation, no pixie magic or misfortune or trial—has ever changed, nor will it *ever* change, that fact."

I almost wasn't sure it was myself that had spoken.

"And—what did you say to her at the time?" Miss Red prompted. "Did you say that?"

I coughed.

"Well—did you say something *like* that, at least?"

I drained my teacup in one draught.

"Sir Rowan . . . tell me you said *something*, at least?"

"I said nothing," I rasped finally. "My lady's wish was that I leave."

The shop bells rang out once more, interrupting what might otherwise have been an extremely uncomfortable moment.

"Re-ed!" The voice of the Pomegranate Café's mistress, Miss Sakura, carried over the shelves. Tucked into the corner as we were, we could not yet see her. "I know you aren't closed yet, it's only four in the afternoon. I'm coming in, okay? I brought you some chai. There's some Midsummer things I want to go over, and then you will not *believe* who came in today asking for a date!"

Five

Dragon Woes

⁓⬥⬥⬥⁓

Daisy

I wish I was stronger—really, I do.

That was what I was thinking as I flew back home after talking to Sakura. Maybe it seems like a funny thing for a dragon to think? A funny thing, too, for a recluse who's just managed not only to go out in public, but also has made plans to go out in public *again*.

But I'm not strong. Not deep down, in the darkest part of my soul. There, very far inside—a place I can never show the pixies—there, I am terrified that I will never quite do things right. That I will never know what I need, much less have the courage to ask for it.

My mother used to tell me that strength was quiet, and strong, and solid. When she said that, I would always think of the Tree that keeps the pixies alive. In their hollow under the mountain, you see, there is a magical Tree—sort of a Tree of Knowledge, or a Tree of Life. There are all kinds of myths about Trees like that. They live forever, and they're so alive and so steeped in magic that they glow, and make everything around them bloom. That's what I imagined strength to be.

But when I got older and took on my role as Guardian, I realized that the pixies have a kind of strength too. They are very little, and very weak, it's true—they're only the size of my palm when I am human, and they fly around on gossamer wings like so many dragonflies. They hate the cold and they fear change and they are always terribly worried about something, or terribly excited. And yet—they go on. They live lives full of drama and nerves, and they embrace it all.

But I often forget how little everyone else knows about them. I suppose in order to understand why I made the mistakes I did, it might help to know their story . . . Besides, it shows how important Midsummer and fire divination is to the pixies.

Pixies never write anything down, so instead they tell each other this tale endlessly. It comes in a lot of variations, I guess because it's been centuries now since these events actually happened. I know Rhys had collected some versions of it, but I've never shared the full story before, now that I think of it. But usually, the basic tale goes like this: *Once upon a time there was a pixie queen whose name was Silver-tree, and her daughter, whose name was Gold-tree. On Midsummer, Gold-tree and Silver-tree went into the forest and found a boulder. On top of that boulder there was a magical flame.*

Silver-tree, being a vain queen, saw that this was a magic fire and immediately asked, "Am not I the most beautiful queen in the world?"

"Oh indeed you are not," said the fire. (Probably thinking that it would rather talk about how to get off its boulder rather than how pretty someone may or may not be, I think. But do fires worry about such things?)

Silver-tree didn't take this very well. "Then who is?" she demanded.

"Gold-tree, your daughter," said the flames. (And that is the source of the trouble. Funny how a single perverse remark can be so lasting!)

Silver-tree went home, blind with rage. She sent everyone away and said she had a terrible headache, and vowed she would never be well until she could eat the heart of Gold-tree, the princess.

At nightfall the king came home, and heard that Silver-tree, his wife, was very ill. He went to her room and asked her what was wrong with her.

"Only a thing which you may heal if you like," said she. (Awfully manipulative. I would hate to think I'd ever tricked someone that way.)

"There is nothing at all which I could do for you that I would not do," he promised.

So the queen said, "If I get the heart of Gold-tree to eat, I shall be well."

The king was horrified at this idea, but said he would go away to think about it. Instead, he went straight to his daughter, Gold-tree, and heard the whole story about the magical fire from her. Together, they decided to consult the deity of the pixies, who sometimes goes by the name Bright Wren.

Bright Wren took pity on the king and princess, and told them of a hermit who lived even deeper in the woods. If Gold-tree went and lived with the hermit, then she would be safe. She left without delay, and the king then gave a bird's heart to his wife to eat; and Silver-tree rose well and healthy, and all the fire's damage had been undone.

That is, until a year had passed. On Midsummer Silver-tree went into the forest again, just as she had before, and again she found the magical bonfire. (Because pixies really don't learn their lessons the first time around.)

"Hello fire," said Silver-tree. " Am I not the most beautiful queen in the world?"

"No, you still are not," answered the flames. (Probably mad about still being stuck on a rock.)

"Who else could it be?" asked the queen. (Who had a one-track mind, apparently.)

"Why, Gold-tree, your daughter, is the most beautiful in the world."

"That's impossible," laughed the queen. "One whole year ago, I ate her heart, and her beauty became mine."

"Don't be ridiculous," said the fire. "Gold-tree isn't dead. I saw her just the other day. She is living nearby with a hermit in a cave."

Silver-tree went home, and begged the king to gather a traveling party, and said, "I am going to see my dear Gold-tree, for it is so long since I saw her." The party was arranged, and they went away. (Because the king forgot about why his daughter was gone in the first place? I never have understood this part. But, knowing the pixies as I do, I must admit it is possible.)

It was Silver-tree herself that was at the head of the party, and she led them straight up the mountain in search of the cave. And they might never have found it . . .

But meanwhile Gold-tree was out gathering flowers, because the hermit's cave was nice and hidden but also boring. (A very pixie sentiment.) *As she was in the woods, she heard the sounds of the queen and party coming. She ran back at once to the cave, but not before they caught sight of her.*

"It's awful!" she called to the hermit. "The queen is coming, and she will kill me."

"She will do nothing of the kind," said the hermit. "We will seal you in a cavern where she cannot get near you."

They managed to hide Gold-tree just as the queen and her party arrived. Silver-tree found the cave at last, she began to shout: "Come to meet your own mother, when she comes to see you." But Gold-tree said that she could not, that she was locked in the room, and that she could not get out of it.

Silver-tree was determined, though. "Will you not put out your little finger through the keyhole, so that I may give a kiss to it?" she said.

Gold-tree put out her little finger, and Silver-tree went and put a poisoned thorn in it, and Gold-tree fell down dead. (Pixies don't die of natural causes, so to them this is unimaginably tragic.)

When the hermit realized what had happened, after the queen and her party went away, they were terribly sad. They prayed to Bright Wren, who answered that prayer with a second gift: the seed which could grow a magic tree. (The first gift was, I suppose, the cave. The pixies aren't too bothered about counting things.)

The hermit planted the seed within the cave, and soon a mighty, magical Tree grew. It filled the cave with light and life, until even the rocks glowed and curling vines came out of them. One of these vines grew up and knocked the thorn right out of Gold-tree's finger, and the princess leapt up, alive! In that moment she swore to always look after the Tree that had saved her life.

So Gold-tree and the hermit lived for another year very peacefully, but Silver-tree wasn't done. When the year was out, at Midsummer, she went into the forest once more. There she found the magical fire.

"Show me the most beautiful pixie in the world," she said. (Going for a new variation on the theme?)

The flames sprouted up and, in them, Silver-tree saw her daughter, Gold-tree, still alive and well and living with the Tree in the hermit's cave.

Without another word the queen went to her people, and prepared to march up the mountain once more. But this time, there was another pixie on the mountain too, who had come to pay Midsummer respects to the flame. This pixie was a priestess, and she knew better than to ask the fire silly questions. Instead she looked in it and saw her destiny.

When Silver-tree came to the cave and offered her daughter a drink, the priestess was there. She took the drink, which Silver-tree said was only harmless water from the lake, and tossed it onto the magic fire. The flames went black and then died. Silver-tree, whose plan to poison Gold-tree had been thwarted, vowed revenge and stormed back down the mountain.

Gold-tree and the hermit were very happy. But the priestess said only, "I have done my good work for you, and now I must go away."

"Please, you must stay," said Gold-tree. "The queen has said that she will come again, and we need your help to stay safe!"

So the three pixies prayed to Bright Wren together, and together they received the third gift, a shining egg which the deity pulled from the ashes of the magical fire. From this egg hatched a dragon. Gold-tree and her friends helped the dragon grow up fast and strong so that it would help them scare away Silver-tree and anyone else who came to harm them.

That's usually where the pixies end the story. It either leaves them feeling a little thrilled and anxious, like an old ghost story—because the silver pixies *do* still live in Belville, and might one day show up at the cave—or sometimes they tell it in a jovial way, and they rejoice, saying, *and that dragon was you, Daisy!* Of course, it wasn't actually me—it was one of my ancestors. This *is* a very old story, after all. It's been so long since that time that no one even recalls if the story is true. In fact, back in the spring, my pixies—led by Goldy, Bree, and Sha—made peace with the "silver" pixies in Belville, and all is forgiven.

But they still get a slightly spooky feeling around Midsummer.

In any case, for all their stories and noise and inconstancy, they are strong, too. They believe in gifts and fate, and they feel very secure in their lovely home.

I am not like that. I just can't accept that *fate* is all there is, somehow, and that's part of what made me worry that I was holding Rhys back. Maybe it's because I'm supposed to look after the pixies, so I'm always on the lookout for danger. Somehow though I became even *more* worried after the pixies all made peace. I just felt listless and *not enough*—and I don't think it's something a magical fire could fix.

I'm not trying to say I'm unhappy, because I always knew what my role would be. I always knew my mother would leave, as her uncle did before her, and that my brothers would too. Something came to them, some instinct that said it was time to go, and so they left. That's how it must go—after all, a whole family of nearly immortal dragons living on one little mountain would soon ruin any chance the pixies had of hiding. There really is only room for one. And that one is me, and the pixies are very happy with that, and so I do my best.

But . . . even though I know I must stay, I *want* to stay . . . I've always felt like I was looking for something I couldn't find. Something I didn't have the strength to find.

Visiting Sakura and hearing her Midsummer plans stirred all this up for me, I think. But even distracted as I was, I got home well before sunset. The summer was still young, just present enough that the evening was long and warm, but all the baby animals were not quite out of their nests and dens. It was quiet. I rested on a rock overlooking the waterfall that hides the pixies' home.

Even though technically the pixies didn't have to hide any more, they liked it there. *I* liked it there. The Tree is in a cave deep in the mountain, of course, and surrounding it are caverns where the pixies and I live, but lately I'd spent more and more time outside. The mouth of the cave was behind the waterfall, but in front of the waterfall was a lovely little garden. It wasn't always that way—actually, Rhys helped me set it up. The pixies mostly just watched. Funny as it may seem, I've always loved gardening. It's even how I met Lavender and Rhys in the first place—though that's a long story.

Anyway, my new garden in front of the pixies' home was my pride and joy. There's a cliff on either side of the waterfall, you see, and the two walls curve around and sink back into the forest, and that creates a sheltered glen. It used to be totally wild, but with Rhys's help I cleared out the undergrowth and had been growing flowers there, in amongst the boulders and all around the edges of the waterfall's pond. Wildflowers of all kinds, foxgloves and mosses and ferns in the shady areas around the walls, and poppies and lavender and sunflowers out in the light. And meadowsweet, just like Sakura had mentioned. *Come to think of it, I never did give her an answer about using the flowers for her party . . .*

But in my garden, even no answer felt like an answer, somehow. And just being out in nature is party enough, I think! The pixies adored it. In fact it was often teeming with activity—just not any knights.

Looonely. That was what the rushing waters seemed to say.

I tried to ignore it—I thought instead about what the pixies would say, the Elders especially. That's Goldy and Bree, and Sha. They take the most interest in my affairs. They'd been the ones to tell me to seek out friendship in town—a startling idea in itself. Just two years ago, not one of the pixies would have *ever* suggested that I leave the Tree, even for an afternoon.

But ever since they met Rhys, they've been more open. They'd probably adore Sakura's party idea, just like they love telling fairy tales and giving gifts and talking about divinity and *love.*

And I . . . I like that kind of talk.

But liking it doesn't mean I'm good at it. I only ever expected to be a Guardian. I never expected to be someone's love. And then of course when I had a chance, I went and fell in love with the one kind of person who should *never* be associated with a dragon—a knight! It was doomed from the start. But I don't want doom. I want magic, like what the pixies talk about.

I want something that will help me become strong.

I want to find what's *right.*

Six

Worst Dinner Date Ever

Rhys

I do not, quite honestly, remember very much more of that afternoon. However I do recall Miss Red and Miss Sakura following me to the tavern that evening. It was a short walk under the trees of the town's central park, and yet it was far, far too long.

"I should have known what was going on when he started walking off in *this* direction every night," Miss Red said to her friend as they crossed Market Square behind me. Even the shops lining the park seemed to listen in.

"This isn't a time for 'should's. This is a time for intervention," Miss Sakura whispered back. No doubt her voice could have carried over the peaked roofs and all the way into the forest beyond.

For perhaps the first time, I wasn't sure if I was agitated that they considered themselves so involved—or relieved.

I had intended to eat at the bar and then retire to my room, as had become my habit. Instead I found myself seated at a table amid the noise and bustle of the tavern's main floor. Madame Lavender's tavern is truly the bedrock of Belville, and its constant business attests to that fact. Laughter and chatter filled the central room up to its wooden rafters, and magical fires sparkled in their hearths at either side of the room, despite the summer heat. Quaint as it might have been, I admit I did not find it pleasant. Miss Sakura, Miss Red, and William were staring at me over soup and salad as though I might explode at any moment.

If I could, perhaps I would.

As I did my best to *not* think about my lady and how I'd introduced her to tavern food a year ago and she'd been so delighted that my heart literally felt like it had cracked open, Misses Red and Sakura made plans.

"You can't keep playing the tragic hero," said Miss Red.

"Though you do it very well," said Miss Sakura, eyeing my uneaten food.

"You know better than anyone that you have to *act*," Miss Red insisted.

"Aren't knights supposed to be brave?" added Miss Sakura.

"You're just going to have to gather your courage and *talk to her*," they said together.

"Can't you let the poor man eat?" said William.

I couldn't possibly have stomached a bite.

The problem was, I knew they were right. But when I offered this to Miss Red as a compromise, she saw right through it.

33

"Saying 'you're right' doesn't mean you're going to do anything," she said, waving a fork in my direction. "It's not me you should be talking to, it's Daisy."

Therein lay the issue. At last, I pushed my plate away. "I can not very well speak to her if she doesn't wish me to."

"How about you let me set you up?" Miss Sakura suggested. "It'd give you the perfect opportunity. And I really think—"

"No," I interrupted. "If my lady had wished to see me, she would have said so. She did not. I will not disrupt her intentions for her—her evening at the café."

"It's a date," Miss Sakura said pointedly. "And if you aren't there, then I'll find someone else to be."

"Someone else is what my lady asked for," I reminded her through gritted teeth.

"Hardly. You didn't hear her list of specifications." Miss Sakura was cut off from saying more, possibly because Miss Red elbowed her. Had I gritted my teeth any harder, they might have split.

"If you won't talk to her on a date, then maybe you should come up with another excuse," Miss Red suggested.

"Or no excuse at all," Miss Sakura conceded. "Just go up and talk to her. Aren't you basically the only person in town who knows how to find her?"

"She will come down when she is ready," I said.

"She just did," Miss Sakura said, gesturing out the tavern's open door in the direction of her café. "She's ready—she just doesn't know it yet."

"I will wait until she *knows*."

"Sir Rowan." Miss Red interrupted her friend's enthusiasm once more, this time with a brush of her hand against my arm. My arms which were, I realized, very firmly crossed over my

34

chest. As I endeavored to act a *little* more civilized, Miss Red went on, "The thing is, Daisy isn't a mind-reader. If she brought this whole expectations thing up and you never *said* anything, and you *still* haven't said anything, then she might take that as a sign that you're happier alone. She might think you have no real interest in being together."

I must admit—this truth had never occurred to me. It was a revelation of the worst kind. *Surely,* I thought, *surely, my lady would know me better than that . . .*

But would she? After all, I hadn't always been forthright with exactly how I felt. Not the details, at least. And sometimes, not even the broad strokes . . .

Did all of this happen because I was never honest enough with her?

My stomach flipped; it was a good thing I hadn't eaten.

"I'm sure you were always very good to her, Sir Rowan," Miss Sakura added more gravely. "But that's part of the problem with being a knight, right? She might have thought part of it was just due to good manners."

Another terrible blow. Vaguely, in the back of mind, a part of me *had* always wondered . . . Especially because my poor lady could never forget I had once been a knight; how could she, when all her life she'd been afraid of dragon hunters and knights in general . . .

"And the knight thing caused more problems than just that, didn't it," Miss Sakura added once more.

I set my elbow on the table and my head in my hand.

"It's not like he can just *not* be a knight," William said, in my defense.

"I would if I could," I whispered. That refrain—how long had it been lurking in my heart? Years; even before I met my lady.

35

I would be anything else if I could . . .

But at the very core of the matter, I had never had the strength to even try to be anything else.

"It's also not like she's scared of him," Miss Sakura replied, glancing at me. "Right?"

"Never," I answered, horrified at the very thought. "My lady is more powerful than I could ever dream of being."

"So there you have it, then," said the shadow witch. "If you're both able to have a reasonable conversation about it, then why not try?"

She dug into her noodles with an air of satisfaction, a job well done. But I was still in turmoil.

"We might have to take some baby steps first," Miss Red said, still looking at me.

"You're sure you don't want to be her date?" Miss Sakura asked. When I shook my head, she tilted hers, thinking. "Okay, then. I can't tell you what to do, Sir Rowan—but I *will* tell you this. The café is hosting a Litha party, and we're using meadowsweet from the pixies' garden. Why don't you be the one to collect it and deliver it to the café? That way Daisy doesn't have to come all the way down here if she doesn't want to, and it's not like you'll get lost, since you've been to see the pixies before. I'll even pay you for your trouble."

I wrinkled my nose. I doubted *anything* Miss Sakura could pay me would be enough to compensate for whatever meddling she had planned. Most Midsummer traditions I could think of included reckless abandon like playing with fire, indulging pixies' pranks, and worse—inviting deities of woods and abundance into homes, where they could not be counted on to abide by proper rules. In a word, it struck me as dangerous. Magic is rife at solstice celebrations.

And yet . . . if Daisy had agreed to be part of it . . .
There wasn't any way I could say no.

Seven

A New Friend

Daisy

Sakura had told me to come by the café for tea several days later, and she'd have someone there for me to meet. That's all.

To be honest, it's probably a good thing that that's all she told me. That way, I didn't have anything to tell the pixies, for them to obsess over. And—there wasn't really anything for me to obsess over, either. My only option was to turn up or not.

Let me tell you, I had *so* many doubts. It was honestly harder to go to the café that day than it was to face down angry dragons. And I have done that, by the way. I think at that moment, I would have gladly taken the rampaging dragon.

But that's just being silly, I tried to remind myself. After all, I had *asked* Sakura to set me up on a date. And I prepared as best as I could, which mostly meant I let the pixies help me choose something to wear—not too fancy, but not my usual smudged gardener's overalls or grass-stained dresses, either. Before I met Rhys, I really just used human form to tend to my plants. Now here I was seeking out human society, and in a new beaded top and clean shorts, even.

Well, in any case, of course there wasn't anything to worry about, really. Sakura had taken care of all that. Everything about the Pomegranate Café was reassuring. Even the wood paneling on the outside is painted a calm sort of plum pink, with clean white trim and charmingly uneven roof lines and windows. The patio in front filled with inviting furniture and even a weatherproof box of books, and I might have simply stayed out there if it hadn't been full of diners already. But the moment I opened the door of the café—even before I was over the threshold—the shadow witch took my hand in hers.

"Daisy, right on time! I set up a special table for you. There's no need to order, all you have to do is be your lovely self. Glacial, I'm going upstairs now!" Sakura called over her shoulder as she pulled me straight to the unveiled stairs at our right.

Glacial—the other employee at the café, someone I hadn't ever met—didn't respond, but there was a flurry of activity behind the sales counter, set back along the left wall. In fact, the whole café was full of activity. Each little table and even the sofas under the front windows seemed full of people, and they all were talking, so much that for a moment I felt like even the antique teapots lining the shelves on the walls were yelling out for my attention. It was all very warm and cozy, of course, but all so *much*. I tugged at Sakura's hand. "We're going upstairs? Am I going with you?"

"Of course you are." Sakura released my hand, but turned

to give me a friendly smile. She climbed the stairs carefully, holding quite close to the rail, so I followed suit. Thankfully, the higher we rose, the more the noise of the main floor faded. "I thought, this is perfect. You two will be the very first people to use the seating on the balcony. Plus, it'll be a little quieter, and you won't have to worry about being crowded. I still haven't opened up the second floor to the public—so you're getting a special preview! You'll have to let me know what you think of the hanging flower pots I added. And don't worry, because I'll be able to see you from the counter just fine in case anything goes wrong. Which it won't."

"I'm not worried," I told her as we neared the top, although I definitely was. But I could see she'd put a lot of thought into this, and I trusted her insight. She'd already thought of things I never would have remembered. "Um—there *are* two of us, then? You did find someone?"

"Did I ever! Daisy, I didn't just find someone. He was banging down my door looking for the opportunity. Weren't you?" Sakura beamed as she turned at the top of the stairs and addressed a stranger sitting at the one set table along the balcony railing.

"You certainly could say that," the stranger answered, with an easy smile and the kind of gallantry that instantly reminded me of Rhys. I had to cling to the railing for a moment because it felt like the polished wood floor beneath us was spinning.

"Daisy, this is Hunter. He does all our specialty tea and spice supply. Hunter, Daisy is a dear friend and I insist you treat her to a nice, fun afternoon. Maybe you can tell her your secrets of the trade; after all, she's agreed to supply the café with some pixie magic and meadowsweet for our Litha party. Haven't you, Daisy?" Sakura asked, reaching out to guide me to a seat.

I couldn't recall if I'd actually agreed to that. I also didn't want her to notice how much my hands were trembling. In the end I mumbled something affirmative and just brushed her fingers with mine, collapsing at last into my chair.

If Sakura noticed any of this, she said nothing. Instead she continued twinkling cheerfully as she told us, "There's rose green tea in the pot, and honey beside it. I had Glacial make up some special scones for you both, and I myself made the tea sandwiches. I'll be back later to check on you and bring up some dessert, if you want any. Now, be good!"

Sakura sailed off, and for a moment, the homey atmosphere of the Pomegranate Café descended over me. Hunter was quiet at first while he poured us both some tea. Our balcony wrapped around the Pomegranate Cafe, hugging the wall. It didn't quite meet up with the tall windows framing the front door, but there was plenty of light from a series of floral chandeliers. Around us, more chairs and tables stood silently, waiting. I took the opportunity to breathe deeply—something I'm always reminding the pixies to do, so I may as well try it myself, I figured. And I just watched him. Even if he was gallant, he really didn't look anything like Rhys.

Not that I'm here to think about Rhys. Focus, Daisy!

When I'm in human form, I look human. I'm just a little tall and pale and usually freckled or sunburnt, that's all. Hunter, on the other hand, didn't look human one bit. That is, he had all the necessary human features—skin, light brown; eyes, dark green; mouth, smiling slightly; hands, calloused—but there was an air about him that just *wasn't*. It wasn't mortal at all. He did have deep green hair curling over his collared shirt, and a pair of antlers rising from his head, but that wasn't quite it. There was something very ancient about the way he moved.

So Sakura took what I said seriously, I thought, still watching him. I wondered vaguely if I ought to be worried. In all my years as a Guardian for the pixies, I'd gotten used to measuring up anyone I met. Hunter was one of the few people I'd come across who seemed like he'd be more powerful than me, and I couldn't quite figure out why.

But of course, I reminded myself, we weren't out on the mountain or anywhere near the Tree. We were in the middle of Belville, in the Pomegranate Café, and a powerful witch was watching us. We couldn't have been safer. Besides, the way Hunter passed me my cup and the honey was completely amiable, like at any minute he'd shrug and say, *funny how things end up, isn't it?*

Without fully meaning to, I let the tension ease out of my shoulders. *So far, so good,* I thought. *Hopefully he hasn't even noticed my nerves.*

Hunter sipped from his cup and tilted his head, green eyes lit up from within. He smiled crookedly at me as he said, "Bit soon for you to be out looking for dates, isn't it, my friend?"

Eight

An Unknown Face

Rhys

I was *not* "staking out" the Pomegranate Café.

I do happen to work right *next* to the café, as anyone can tell you. So out of necessity, I must pass by the institution on occasion. I can't help it if I notice who goes in and out. Knights—*good* knights, anyway, not that there are very many of those—must be observant if they wish to live beyond their first year of service. If anything, it's Miss Sakura's fault for attracting such beautiful clientele.

And then setting said clientele up on ill-advised *dates.*

Needless to say, my mood was not sunny when I returned to Red's Alchemy & Potions with a late lunch from the nearby diner for myself and William.

Miss Red was out gathering the last of the spring moss for her growth potions, and the afternoon was especially fine; most, if not all, of Belville's population was out-of-doors. Those who did not crowd Market Square crowded the shores of the lake at the town's outskirts, or went for short hikes on the mountain. Thus William and I had the shop to ourselves. A reprieve that should have been welcome, after the bustle of the morning.

We sat side by side behind the sales counter as we ate our sandwiches, as has become our custom during my time working for Miss Red. William allowed me to spend several quiet minutes stabbing at the slice of pickle that accompanied my sandwich with a slender salad fork before he made comment.

"So," he said, having wolfed down the majority of his sandwich already, "did you see the guy?"

There are those who mistake my manners for arrogance. But I am not above admitting the truth, when indeed it *is* true. Therefore I will confess I met this question with something far less than equanimity. In fact, I scowled.

"I did not see a *guy*," I informed William. "I merely happened to see my—Miss Daisy entering the café."

"Did she see you?"

"She did not." And, knowing what even the staunchest of allies would ask next, I added, "I did not think it the right moment to talk to her."

"Uh huh."

"She is obviously busy."

"True."

"She might have had an appointment with Miss Sakura."

"Yeah."

"After all, Miss Sakura told me herself that she wishes to deal with m—Miss Daisy in a professional capacity."

44

"Also true. Meadowsweet, and other flowers too, it sounds like."

"That is my understanding as well. Of course—" I paused. My pickle was now a mangled heap of vinegary seeds. There is a limit for everyone, and I had reached mine. "*Is* today the day of her date?"

William, who had been snuffling the remains of his cloth sandwich wrapper, looked up at me for a moment before responding. On our initial evening with Miss Red and Miss Sakura, I had refused to be told any details pertaining to my lady's arrangement. The knowledge, I thought at the time, would only prove torturous. However, now that the moment was upon us—potentially—I found I could not stand the suspense.

"Yeah," William said eventually. His manner was half apologetic, half cautious. I suppose I *was* suddenly itching to draw my sword.

But the weapon is purely ceremonial at this point.

"Saki's got everything under control," William continued. Looking away, in a quieter voice he added, "You don't know him."

"I don't know him?" This did not make me feel remotely better. Belville is not a large town. I'd lived there long enough to know everyone and then some. "Where, in the names of the gods and goddesses, did she conjure this man up from, then?"

William glanced at me and sneezed. A habit when he finds something unreasonable, I have observed. "She didn't conjure him. He does business with the café."

This also did not make me feel better. "*What kind of—*"

"Tea. He delivers their tea, okay? He's been dropping by pretty regularly now for the past few months."

I'm not sure what I was doing, but I stopped it to consider this. *Tea delivery* was unexpected. It sounded almost civil. "He is . . . a postman?"

William snorted, another habitual sound, this one closer to a laugh. "Not exactly. He goes out and gathers it himself, see. He's a specialist. That's how Glacial's always baking up exotic things in her cupcakes."

"Then why doesn't he date Glacial?" I asked, sour as my ruined pickle.

"Could *anyone* date Glacial?" William mused, before shaking his floppy ears. "I don't think she's into that. Anyway . . ."

The silence was laden with such platitudes as *it will all work out* and *well, anyway, he isn't you.*

I began stabbing my sandwich. "William," I said. "You know I hold you in the highest esteem. You have ever been a knowledgeable and dependable presence. However, if you tell me now that I shouldn't worry myself . . ."

William shook his ears again, and huffed. "Well, actually, maybe you *should.*"

Nine

Selfish Truths

❧

Daisy

"Wh-what?" I sputtered, barely catching my tea in my napkin. "How—how did you know? Did Sakura say something?"

"All Saki said was that she needed help," Hunter told me with that same gentle, half-amused smile. His eyes slid down to the counter below us as he added, "And that she wanted to help me."

"Help—how? Oh, dear." In my haste to recover myself, I'd managed to knock my cup over entirely. As I did my best to mop up the mess, I continued rambling. "I'm so sorry—I'm really not sure how I could help you—I never meant to bother her—really, if this is all an inconvenience—"

"Hey." Hunter placed his napkin over mine, and he waited

until I looked up. When I finally did, his eyes had deepened somehow, that kind of reassuring green that comes in the living growth of spring. Honestly, looking at him in that moment was a little like sitting at the base of the Tree. I stared, mesmerized, as he went on. "It's no inconvenience, Daisy. You can relax. I don't intend to say anything to her. And I'm not here to judge you, or take anything from you. I'm just here for the tea. And maybe the conversation.

"This could be good, actually," he added as he sat back, releasing me. I blinked down at my hands. The mess from the spilled tea was all gone. My napkin was dry.

Slowly, still a little in shock, I tucked my napkin back into my lap. This time, I reached out to pour another cup of tea myself. As I did, I thought through what he'd said. "You think meeting with me could be a good thing?"

"I think you're due for a break, Daisy," he answered lightly. "And I'm glad you've decided to stay."

Have I? Well, I had fresh tea in my cup, so I supposed I had. I watched him for another minute, wondering if this was also his doing. But I felt quite normal—a little nervous, even, and that was perfectly normal too. *I did decide to put myself out there,* I reminded myself. *And he seems like he has something to say.*

"Rhys—that is—the relationship you alluded to—it wasn't bad, if that's what you mean by needing a break," I told him as I took a cucumber sandwich from the tray between us.

A completely un-tea-soaked sandwich. But I decided not to think about that. My heart was muddled enough without bringing questions about magic into the mix.

"I didn't think so. Seems to me that the one being hard on you is yourself," Hunter said, taking two sandwiches in his turn.

"I . . . I suppose I can't argue with you," I said, thinking it over. "It's a—a habit, you could say."

"It usually is. Especially with people who feel that they have an important duty to fulfill." For just a moment, just a very brief moment, I thought he might have winked. "That's why I'm here, then. Let's give you something else to focus on."

"Something—like what?"

"Why don't you tell me about this Rhys?"

"I shouldn't have shared that name. It's private," I said automatically. "I—I'm sorry. I'm not sure how much I should say."

"Alright, then. Tell me something else." Once more, his gaze seemed to drift downward—and once more I wondered if I'd imagined it. "Is it difficult, letting yourself trust someone, when you have such a strong protective instinct?"

I set down my sandwich. I could feel my cheeks getting hot again. I *do* have a very strong instinct for protection—perhaps you've noticed, and I'm sure by now you know why. I just hadn't ever realized how obvious it was. There had never been anyone to call me out on it, I suppose. "Is it—well—yes, you could say it is," I admitted quietly. "You see, it isn't just about me."

This time, Hunter's green eyes were fixed on mine. Not mesmerizing, just steady. "No, Daisy. Sometimes it *is* just about you."

"I'm afraid I—I don't know what you mean," I stammered.

"I have a feeling that for our man in question, he who shall not be named, everything comes down to *you*." Hunter tilted his head again, smiling. "But that doesn't always make things easier, does it?"

"It—um—it doesn't." I bit my lip. When we were together, Rhys had sometimes given me that idea—that he was thinking only of me. I assumed at first that such behavior just came naturally to knights. And of course it was flattering. But . . . it was also what scared me. What if he let his life become so small, *too* small, only as big as the pixies and the Tree and me, and then some day he came to regret it? What if it was only his kindness that gave me that impression in the first place? How could someone so accomplished and so strong be meant to live with just *me*?

As I thought this over, Hunter had pulled a scone from the stack and broke off a piece. "Hmm, she figured out just what to do with that dark moon basil, then," he said, mostly to himself. Noticing my gaze, he gestured toward the scones and added more clearly, "It's worth trying one. These are good."

To my surprise, I'd already finished my sandwich. As I picked out a scone and buttered it, I admitted, "All the best things I've eaten have been from Sakura's café. I—I don't get out very much."

"You don't need to. That's why Saki has me bring exotic things here," Hunter told me. This time I knew for sure he winked.

As I tried the scone, I remembered Sakura saying something very similar. *By all means, keep being a recluse.* But the pixies had been so insistent I go make friends . . .

Well, these things will develop in time, I thought. I glanced at the herbed scone in my hands, wondering if my sense of ease was due simply to good food.

"And you, I understand, are also supplying the café?" Hunter asked. He sounded gently amused rather than upset by the idea, but I admit I frowned.

"In a manner of speaking, I guess I am—but only for Litha," I said. "And not for tea. It's just—something Sakura came up with, the meadowsweet, I mean."

"It's not a bad idea," Hunter said thoughtfully. "Long evenings are perfect for dreams, and love abounds in the summer. But why wouldn't you supply the café with other things as well, Daisy? You mustn't think I fear the competition."

"No—I didn't necessarily think that. It's just that I'd never thought about it, really. I like growing the flowers, no matter what they are. I hadn't ever given thought to . . ."

"What comes next?" Hunter tilted his head as he looked at me, like he knew that the answer was right but also that it didn't make sense. And he had a point. Here I was, worrying about the future in all kinds of ways—and yet I'd never given a thought to the future of my garden, or its produce.

"I guess not," I admitted, smiling a little at myself.

"Well, there's nothing wrong with that. Our friends the pixies never do worry about the future, do they, unless it's shown to them," he said with familiar humor.

I hesitated. His comment was just enough like the pixies' tale about Silver-tree that at first I wondered if it was a threat.

But then he leaned back and laughed. "Don't worry, I didn't mean anything by it. Only that visions aren't always the gifts they seem to be. And sometimes . . . Sometimes they are unnecessary. Don't you think?"

Thoughts of the pixies and their fairy tales faded, replaced by a sudden wonder: *what would I see in the flames, if I went looking for my true love?* I had a sneaking suspicion that Hunter was right. I might not need to look . . .

"I guess it might be nice, though," I sighed, "to be certain."

Hunter tipped his head again, as though considering this, but said nothing. I lapsed back into thought, feeling just a little silly. Like a mythological pixie queen asking who the most beautiful person in the world might be. *Am I asking the wrong questions, somehow?*

"Certainty aside, what would you *like* to do, Daisy?" Hunter asked, reclaiming my attention.

"Well—I'm really not sure. So much is changing, or has changed. I don't know exactly how I'm going to fit any more. I mean, I know I don't fit into my old life. I'm just not sure what my new life should look like." I hesitated, realizing belatedly, "I'm sorry, did you mean this afternoon? Because I—I should be getting back—"

Hunter laughed, and somehow it sounded just like trees in the wind, or water over rocks. "Never mind what I meant. Saki would tell you never to worry about 'should,' my friend."

"Would she?" *I haven't spoken enough to her,* I thought. And then I thought about that thought. *Maybe the pixies weren't entirely wrong, telling me to go out.*

"Patience," said Hunter, his eyes still dancing with that laugh, "takes a special kind of strength. Don't you think so?"

"Ugh," I said, without thinking about it. Then immediately I flushed.

"Do not apologize," Hunter insisted, laughing again. "You're right. I like you, Daisy. I wouldn't mind doing this again."

His words were warm, and in a rush they made me think of Red, and Sakura, and Lavender and Officer Thorn. *Friends. Maybe?* "Do you—do you come here with deliveries often?" I asked cautiously.

"Reasonably so," he answered, still smiling. "In fact, for the next few days, I'll be sticking around. After our talk today, I have half a mind to join in this party Saki's throwing. You don't mind if I do a bit of gathering up on the mountain, do you?"

"Of course, I couldn't tell you not to," I said carefully,

wondering once more how much Sakura might have told him. Most people in Belville knew about me, of course. But I never talked to most people in Belville, so I wasn't sure exactly what line to take now.

That said, he does seem to know an awful lot about the pixies . . .

"I won't go anywhere I'm not supposed to," Hunter assured me with that level, knowing gaze. "You don't last long in my profession without learning that skill, and quick. I only got it wrong once."

This time I was certain his gaze flicked down to the counter below, where Sakura and Glacial worked. I thought I understood a little of the wisdom in his voice. After all, I'd first met Rhys because I'd ventured outside of my normal duty. "Sometimes getting it wrong isn't so bad."

Ten

How to Eat a Cupcake

Rhys

I will no longer deny that I was overly interested in my lady—in Miss Daisy's—movements in town. Doing so has proved futile and, I fear, rather tiring.

To say that I found myself at the Pomegranate Café later that afternoon, then, needs no explanation.

"Here to see me?" Miss Sakura asked, as I lingered beside the sales counter with a mug of lapsang souchong in my hands.

I shook my head. I wasn't there to see anyone, particularly. I knew Miss Daisy had already left. William had noticed her going, and perhaps that is why he'd given me leave to finish work early.

"Well, then, take a seat and stop moping," Miss Sakura

directed, shooing me toward one of the couches or tables strewn haphazardly throughout the café. "I can't stand you lingering about like a gargoyle when I'm supposed to be wiping down these counters. Red must have the patience of a saint. Now, I'm not saying you have to leave, mind you. It *is* near closing time, but I'll be around awhile—Mel and Ryu are coming in to talk about the decorations for Litha. So you're free to sit as long as you like. Just keep your moping to yourself unless you want me to help you *do* something about it."

The last thing I wanted was for Miss Sakura to decide I needed help.

I took the seat farthest away from the sale counter—a faded paisley couch tucked into the corner beneath one of the front windows. From there, I could see that most of Miss Sakura's patrons had already left for the day. Perhaps it was partly an effect of my mood, but it seemed that the café had become much more mellow than it was during peak hours; the afternoon light through the windows was shadowy, and idle chatter had given way to the *chink* of glasses in the wash and some faint music that Miss Sakura had no doubt set up on a magic speaker somewhere. It was very pensive.

As I watched, Miss Sakura made her way to a table at the back. A low rumbling indicated that her brother, Mister Ryuko, and the café's event planner, Miss Emmelayne, had come in through the kitchen and met her there. In the wake of this disturbance, a diminutive baker trailed about the room.

I had heard, of course, of Miss Glacial. We had not yet met; when I was in a relationship with Miss Daisy, I did not spend much time in town . . . and since that relationship had ended, I had spent most of my time in town at the tavern. Or at work. In any case, from what William had told me, it was not Miss

Glacial's way to engage in friendly chit chat. I myself was not feeling up for company, so I was relieved to know that in all likelihood, my silence was safe.

But that was not to be the case. After lingering around the event planners' table with a tray of pastries, Miss Glacial drifted around the empty café, not unlike a bit of wood on a rolling sea. It was only that the colors were reversed: Miss Glacial's skin is a pale blue, her hair a pale purple, and she was wearing an apron of aquamarine, while the café floor and furniture around her was maple and oak, much of it the product of Mister Ryuko's carpentry. I was just thinking that Miss Glacial looked like she might be swept away by the tide when she spotted me in the corner.

At once, she came over and set her tray on the coffee table before me. What I had at first mistaken for wispiness was in fact wiriness: her presence was solid and undeniable. "Someone's got to eat them," she said simply.

"They look lovely," I told her—reluctantly, because I would have rather moped in silence—but honestly, because they were perfect vanilla cakes with piped yellow and pink frosting, and little white sugar flowers. *Sugared violets from the pixies' garden would go perfectly on those,* I thought, and my stomach soured. "But I'm afraid I really could not eat."

When was *the last time I ate?* I wondered. Had it been long enough that my body and strength had suffered? I couldn't be sure; I hadn't been paying attention.

Miss Glacial put her hands on slim hips as she considered the cupcakes, then me. Behind her, a scaly white tail swished, and patterns of small white scales spread across the backs of her hands and her throat, almost like protective tattoos. Such characteristics often are evidence of dragon magic in the blood, but I chose not to think about that. I did not know Miss Glacial's heritage, nor her intentions. She glanced at the upper level of the café, its tables just as silent and empty as the ones on the ground floor. To my distress, she then sat on the sofa across from me.

"I don't know you," she said. Technically, she said it to one of her cupcakes as she selected it from the tray. But since this was a patently ridiculous thing for her to say to a baked good she herself had created, I assumed the comment was directed at me. She continued to address her cupcake as she sat back and went on, "But Saki talks. I'm sorry."

I would have done my best to be polite—truly, I would have—but everything about this comment made me scowl. "One would think a shadow witch would know something more about discretion."

"Oh, she does," Miss Glacial said, glancing quickly at me. Her eyes were mismatched, one blue, one lavender, echoing her hair. There was a hint of a lopsided smile on her small features as she added, "But she says she hates it when a problem is only a problem because people *don't* talk. That's why she might be hard on you."

"I hadn't noticed," I said stiffly, doing my best not to recall the *gargoyle* remark.

"Hm." Miss Glacial returned her focus to her cupcake. For a moment she seemed to be staring at it intently, and then in one swift, deft movement she separated the lower half of the cake from the whole and then placed it atop the frosting. She noticed me watching this conversion and explained, "Looks prettier the other way round. So that's how we sell them. But it's easier to eat this way."

Undoubtedly she was right; I haven't given much thought

to baked sweets, myself. But two layers of cake sandwiched around frosting did seem more practical than one large lump of frosting and one small lump of cake.

I was still thinking about how easily she had managed the feat with one hand as she held the cake with the other. In my experience, not many people have such fine motor control.

And if they *do* have such control, it's for a reason. Usually a martial one.

"Do you want to talk about what happened?" Miss Glacial once again addressed her dessert. I admit to some surprise—not because she thought the dessert had a story—but because she wanted to continue conversing. "You don't have to. Just, if it helps."

The third surprise came when I realized that actually, I *did* want to talk. It was easier—so much easier—to describe the situation to someone so wholly removed from it. "I came here two years ago last winter," I heard myself say, as if listening to an actor on stage. "Shortly after my arrival, I encountered Miss Daisy in her human form, doing some small service for Madame Lavender. At the time, I was in the company of several other knights who wished to locate the dragon rumored to live atop Belville's mountain. We did not know that the dragon was, in fact, Miss Daisy.

"I fell in love with her before I knew," I said very quietly. "But I always knew there was something special about her. When she told me, it came as no surprise. In fact, I don't believe I could have cared less.

"However, there were the other knights to deal with. The fools went and performed some kind of summoning spell, meant to uncover Miss Daisy's location, which instead brought an uncontrollable ice dragon down upon us all. Naturally this resulted in a series of battles. My own part in this is nothing to be proud of, because truthfully my lady never wanted a battle in the first place, and all the clamor and damage it caused made it necessary for my lady to reveal herself to the town—something she had avoided doing for centuries. But she did so for my sake. And I—I slew the ice dragon, after it had slain my former companions and made it clear that it would do battle with Miss Daisy, too, because she dared to fight alongside knights.

"All was well for a little while," I mused. "However, my lady's duty has always weighed heavily on her, and of course to most, it would be outright heresy to think a knight and dragon might coexist, let alone love. Undoubtedly there have been great pressures upon my lady, many of them because of me and my actions. I was rash in everything I did; unwittingly I unveiled her secret, and I should have suffered consequences for killing that ice dragon. It was not what she wanted. And I—thinking it over now—I can not say that Miss Sakura's unfavorable impression of myself and my problems is wrong."

I looked up to find Miss Glacial deep in contemplation of the last bite of her confection. "*Should* you be punished for killing something that would have killed you and those you love?"

"In the normal course of a knight's quest, you may have a point. But this was not intended to be a battle, it was intended to—to bring a peace, of sorts," I said, unnerved by Miss Glacial's demeanor. It sounded as though the question had some personal meaning for her, and I was not prepared for such a debate. In general, knights are trained to carry out orders rather than question them.

"Finding her wasn't your quest, then?"

"It became that," I said softly. At Miss Glacial's glance, I coughed and added, "It is difficult to explain. I was already a discredited knight then. I did not, and do not, technically answer to a noble family or higher power any more."

"So you can make your own quest."

I must admit, Miss Glacial's interest in questing was starting to unsettle me. *Perhaps I am too old and too sedate for such things now,* I thought. "I would much rather make amends."

"But Saki says you won't talk to her."

I thought about Miss Red, and William, and their insistence on *talking*. "Old habits die hard," I said, at length. "Though I am not a knight in good standing, I have never been brave enough to make a true effort to be anything new. I am not certain how I would go about it. Years in training—years of living by a code—it is not easily abandoned."

"You already *are* something else," Miss Glacial said with that almost childlike simplicity. She handed me a cupcake. "Right? We do get to be more than one thing—don't you think?"

Idly I attempted the maneuver I had seen Miss Glacial perform so easily earlier. It did not come naturally to me; the cake crumbled. But the result was still reasonably effective. "I do not know."

"Me neither." Miss Glacial glanced around the café. "But it seems to work, somehow. Things do change. If you pay attention. What do you think of the lemon in the frosting?"

I looked down and was vaguely shocked to find I'd finished off my cupcake. I took another from the tray and practiced removing the bottom section again. "It is pleasant, but it is overpowering the strawberry and vanilla of the cake."

"Thought so." Miss Glacial looked up at me and, for the first time, she smiled. The effect was like watching fireflies dance in a pastel twilight. "You give much better feedback than Saki. She only knows if she likes it or not. You should come back tomorrow and try the summer berry tortes I'm working on."

"I would be honored," I told her gravely. And though it saddened me that I could not bring the desserts home to share with Miss Daisy, I did feel a glimmer of new hope for the first time.

Eleven

Pixies and Pondering

Daisy

The morning after my date—well, really, just my meeting—with Hunter, some of the pixies wanted to go out and play by the waterfall in the garden, and they wanted me to come. Even now, they didn't quite feel brave enough to go out alone.

Well, the world is an overwhelming place when you are only four inches high, after all. I myself can hardly wrap my head around how big the world must seem to them, especially since in my true form, I'm probably as big as the entire Pomegranate Café.

I suppose they get used to things though, the pixies. I was thinking about that as I lay on the rocks, watching them dance around the droplets of water. I was still puzzling over something I'd admitted to Hunter, about having an 'old' life and now a 'new' life, and wondering where I fit. It was true, even if I hadn't meant to say it. The pixies had made peace with the rest of the world, including the other pixies they'd been hiding from. They didn't really need a guardian any more. And I thought, *for as terrified as the pixies are sometimes of change, they also take to it very gleefully . . .*

"Daisy, Daisy!" they called to me, a little chorus interrupting my thoughts.

I knew what they wanted. I stretched one wing out into the waterfall, so that just the edge met with the cold mountain water. The resulting spray of water delighted them just as much, I think, as the stained-glass colors that turned each droplet into a little piece of rainbow.

I'm not a normal dragon—not really. I spend so much time thinking about the pixies, and wondering about them, that sometimes I forget these basic things about myself! But really, it's no less fascinating than the pixies' history. Dragons come in all colors and types, of course, and they live all across Beyond. Some are fire dragons with bright scales who breathe flame, some are ocean dragons who prefer to swim or blow jets of water. There are rock dragons, and desert dragons, and storm dragons—and ice dragons, too. There are probably many more types I've forgotten, or never knew. I only know about any of them vaguely, the way the pixies know about other kinds of magic, or the way Sakura might know about running different kinds of cafés. There is a worldwide council and a federation of dragons and all that, but I've never dealt with them.

And maybe part of that is *because* my family is a little odd. We do have sharp teeth and claws and scales and tales and the whole bit, of course. My scales are all white. But my wings are not bat-like, the way you might picture other dragons'. Instead, they're more like dragonfly wings, rounded and so thin that the blues and greens and purples of them are see-through in the sunlight. Honestly, they're a lot like pixie wings. Maybe there is a purpose in that. I never thought about it before.

Well, anyway, my point was that it was a little difficult to keep feeling sorry for myself amid the pixies' delight. Not that I *was* sorry, exactly. Except about Rhys.

What I couldn't get out of my head was that first moment, seeing Hunter. The feeling in my stomach when I realized he *wasn't* Rhys. Disappointment. He hadn't felt right.

Of course, everything ended up just fine with Hunter, and he did seem like he might be a good friend. It wasn't that he himself was wrong, in any sense. Just that—he was wrong for *me.*

That's something else I hadn't really thought about. I suppose for most of my life I'd just assumed that *everyone* was wrong. Not because I hate people or anything, but because I was so worried about keeping the pixies safe, and anyone might be a danger to them.

Until that moment looking at Hunter, I'd forgotten just how *right* Rhys felt, when I first let him into my world.

And I had never fully realized how special that feeling was. Maybe, somehow, that feeling in itself was a sort of answer. Maybe, as Hunter had suggested, I really didn't need worries and questions and visions. Maybe . . .

"I shouldn't be thinking about that," I told myself aloud. "I should be thinking about Sakura's meadowsweet."

Everyone else calls her Saki. What if I was close enough to her to do the same? I wondered. *Would that feel right, too?*

"Queen of the Meadow?" a small voice asked, from somewhere just above my head.

I turned and smiled at Goldy, one of the pixies' leaders, hovering in a tiny blur of bright white and yellow sparkle. Though they tell stories about kings and queens, the pixies don't actually have such an organized system of leadership—at least, not any more. And they rarely even refer to themselves by gender or use distinctions like priest*ess* these days. Still, Goldy does have a sort of regal presence, and listened carefully as I said, "I did tell you all about that, didn't I? That Sakura, who runs the Pomegranate Café, would like our permission to use some meadowsweet?"

"You did!" Goldy informed me, twisting gleefully in the air. "But then you didn't talk about it. You haven't talked much lately, Daisy."

This was precisely where most of my recent conversations with the pixies had turned into *you are sad, you should make friends and be happy* lessons. It was a very pixie philosophy, and I didn't begrudge them for that. But I'd also heard it often enough already, so I did my best to head Goldy off. "I've had a lot to think about," I said hastily. "Like wondering how much meadowsweet to take to Sakura, for example."

"What does she want with it?" Goldy asked curiously.

"She wants to use it to celebrate Midsummer," I admitted, a little anxiously. "I think she's going to let people play party games with it, like trying to see the future or predict what their true love might look like."

"Fun!"

And that's precisely why I'd worried. Pixies mean well, but sometimes when they're really excited about a new idea, they can get carried away . . . *and really, if there's* any *truth to the old legend about Silver-tree, what good has looking into magical fires done?*

I suppose it did save Gold-tree in the end, I had to admit to myself.

"You should do it, too, Daisy!" Goldy exclaimed.

I was a little taken aback by this twist. *"Me?* Why, Goldy?"

"You always like to be certain," the pixie said, flying in very close to bop my nose. "Maybe if you see it's just a party game, you won't have to be so certain any more. You can be you!"

I'm accustomed to hearing some pretty random things from pixies, but this stretched my ability to understand. It made so little sense that all I could do was go with it. I shook my head helplessly, laughing a little. "And who is that, do you think?"

"Daisy is our queen," said Goldy by way of answer, sitting atop my head like a crown. "Queen of the garden!"

The other pixies, alerted by Goldy's shout, came over and joined in the game, cheering. Their antics made me laugh—even though, I realized later, I was a little sad not to have had a more serious answer.

Twelve

Inevitable

⚜

Rhys

The day following my conversation with Glacial, I was not
scheduled to work at Red's Alchemy & Potions. Normally, my
free days would have been spent on the mountain . . . Or
perhaps, entirely in Lavender's Tavern.

But I woke that morning determined not to become mired in
such depression. Perhaps it was because I'd come back to the
tavern the night before and eaten my first full meal in weeks.
(Even at the best of times, I have never been accustomed to
eating great quantities of sugar, and eating three cupcakes
didn't sit well with me; the only remedy was to consume actual
nutrition to counteract their effect.) Whatever the reason, I
was up and about in good time. After a ride along the lake,

I felt sufficiently heartened to venture into town, and even to face Miss Sakura again. I had promised Miss Glacial I'd give her my opinion on her tortes, after all, and a promise is a promise—whether or not a shadow witch happens to be involved.

In retrospect, perhaps I should have waited until closing time.

I approached the Pomegranate Café shortly before lunch time. I have always observed a lull in the business at this time, and I had a vague notion that I might somehow deal *only* with Miss Glacial, and not with Miss Sakura at all. However, I should have realized that my luck has never been that propitious.

A large, bright sign placed on the café's modest front patio advertised the upcoming party in honor of Litha. I couldn't help but notice that the advertisement specifically mentioned divination with meadowsweet.

Does Miss Daisy know about that? I wondered. *Or is that shadow witch pressuring her into something without letting her think through all the repercussions?*

If I had to choose a point where it all began, that might be the moment.

To put it another way, before I'd made it through the café door, I was already annoyed with Miss Sakura's meddling, and looking for a fight.

The inside of the café was passably cozy and sparsely populated. As I strode to the counter, however, Miss Sakura was deep in conversation with an unusual individual, and Miss Glacial was nowhere in sight.

"Oh, our knight-errant," said Miss Sakura, as she turned to acknowledge my approach. "Not looking so mopey today—that's good. Your usual lapsang, no sugar?"

"On the contrary," I said, quite firm. "I would like to speak with Miss Glacial, please."

"You would?" It was the stranger, not Miss Sakura, who spoke. The man pivoted to face me, as if he'd been inclined to ignore me before but this mention of Miss Glacial's name was sufficient to claim his attention.

"I would. I have an invitation," I replied, surveying him coolly. This was also a mistake. The moment I met his forest-green eyes, I knew exactly what he was. Ordinarily, as a knight, I would have known better than to stare down such a person. However, I did not appreciate the amusement in his tone.

"She did say you're our resident food critic now." Miss Sakura herself eyed me rather critically. "It might be better if you came back later, though."

"If that is Miss Glacial's opinion then I will respect it," I said politely. "However, I would like to hear it from her."

Miss Sakura, however, was not going to let me pass. "Much as I applaud your interest in conversation all of a sudden, I don't think now's the time."

I frowned. "I must say, Miss Glacial told me about your inclination to *talking*, but still I see no need to be so—"

"Glacial," the stranger interrupted, his amusement shifting into something I should have recognized as dangerous, "is busy."

I drew myself up to my full height, which is not unremarkable. I had at least a foot on Miss Sakura, who was perched on a stool behind the counter. I did not quite measure up to the stranger's antlers, perhaps, but nonetheless I said hotly, "I do not see that *you* are a person who can say if she is busy or not."

"And I do not see that you are in a position to argue with me, Sir Rowan."

"Your knowledge does not frighten me, stranger. Your lack

of manners, however, does."

"This is not the battle you wish to pick, my friend."

"I'll pick whichever battle I like. I do not care for you telling me what I want, or whether my acquaintances are busy, or—"

"Or how your friends might feel?" Miss Sakura interrupted. I stared at her. Her blue eyes were serious, the look of someone who'd struck a blow in order to head off a fight. She'd said the exact thing that I had begun to fear.

"You." The heat had entirely left my voice. It was with cold fury that I addressed her now. "Set. Her. Up. With. *The literal incarnation of—*"

"Just Hunter, please," the stranger interrupted again, holding up a hand.

"I don't care what name you use," I growled before turning back to Miss Sakura. "Do you have any idea how *dangerous—*"

"Daisy is a grownup," the little shadow witch interrupted. "And as I recall, rumor has it she's a lot stronger than you. So I don't see—"

"You don't *see*? She came to you in good faith, and you—you are toying with her. Or worse!"

"I don't need your opinions about how I run my business, Sir Rowan. If you feel so strongly about it, maybe you should think about why you're so willing to talk *about* her and not *to* her!"

I snapped.

I drew my sword.

In retrospect, maybe I should have stopped carrying it after she left . . .

"Well, then," said the stranger, just as I blacked out. "This has been very instructive, don't you think?"

Daisy is a grownup.

She's a lot stronger than you.

Maybe you should think about why you're so willing to talk about her, and never to her.

When I came to, I was sitting beneath a tree. My head was splitting. In fact, it felt like I'd brandished my sword and brought it straight down on my own temple. It took me some minutes to make sense of the fact that I was in Market Square, and that my sword was lying beside me, and that there was no blood or debris on me or my clothes.

"You know," said William, seated beside me, "the first step toward being something other than a knight should probably be *not* trying to solve disputes via sword fight."

"I haven't fought with that thing in ages," I groaned, fighting nausea as I tried to sit upright.

"I know." William panted, watching the café across from us for a moment before adding, "Maybe you should have offered to fix him a drink."

The comment made me laugh weakly, despite everything that weighed on me. Leave it to William—as staunch an ally as there ever could be—to remember that in another life, my specialty was mixing drinks. In fact, that had been part of Miss Red's reasoning for hiring me. She thought my interest in the magic of mixing herbs was not unlike her alchemy.

"Nothing would have done me any good," I reflected. My head was still in my hands, but the world had stopped spinning. "Miss Sakura was right. I am weak."

William cocked his head. "I don't think many of us could stand up to divine magic."

"No one in their right mind would *try*," I amended. "Does this mean you know?"

"About Hunter? Sure. I *am* something of a magical expert,"

71

William reminded me, his panting now resembling a grin. "And if I'd had any doubt, seeing you go flying out of the Pomegranate would have made up my mind. Red was half convinced we ought to close up shop entirely and get you some kind of medical aid. I told her if he'd meant to actually hurt you, then there wouldn't be anything we could do."

After a moment of meditating on this sobering fact, William added, "If I'd've thought you were going to pick a fight with him, I might've warned you."

"It wasn't my intention to pick a fight." I sighed: I knew that wasn't entirely true. "William . . . Tell me honestly. Am I being a complete fool?"

"Honestly?" William stopped panting for a moment, one ear cocked. "Yes. Obviously. I mean, you were just blasted out of a café, and that doesn't happen because you were doing something *smart*. But I wouldn't worry, if I was you. This is only temporary. I know you'll figure it out."

"You . . . know?" I repeated slowly.

"Of course." William shifted closer, his warm fur a reassuring weight against my shoulder. "You're my friend, Sir Rowan. I believe in you."

"Rhys. Call me Rhys," I whispered, my head whirling once more. *My friend.* "And—thank you, William."

"Any time," he replied cheerfully. "Just, you know, maybe try not to get knocked on the head next time, Rhys. Even immortal knights can't take much of that."

Thirteen

Dragons Ahoy!

Daisy

After talking to Goldy, I felt bad, like maybe I was neglecting the pixies. So for the rest of that day I did try to be more sociable, and cheerful . . . but it didn't last too long.

The following day, I felt restless. I couldn't quite figure out why. There wasn't anyone in particular I wanted to see—well, no one I would *let* myself see—but I knew I wanted to see *something*. So after lingering around the Tree in the morning, I finally grew tired of myself and told the pixies I was going out on patrol.

"Out on patrol" sounds very official and it always impresses the pixies—most of them, at least. I think they imagine I soar out around the mountain and find all sorts of villains to head off, right before they find the secret location of the Tree. But there's really no villains on the mountain. Hardly ever, anyway. The only notable ones in centuries had been Rhys and his fellow knights, and they weren't exactly *villains,* although some of them weren't very well-intentioned . . .

Anyway, that was supposed to be the point of Rhys helping me and the pixies become more involved in town life. The other pixies have moved on, and the forest is peaceful, so there really isn't much to fear.

I suppose what I mean is that "patrolling" was really just "flying aimlessly," and flying aimlessly tends to make me feel philosophical. *We* have *made progress since Rhys came,* I was thinking. Of course, the pixies still didn't want anyone to know how to find the Tree, and that made it a little difficult to make true friends in town. However, we'd ended a centuries-long feud and were now officially helping a shadow witch with a *party,* for goodness' sake. It was a far cry from hiding in a cave and pretending we didn't exist.

But what does it mean? That was the question that really plagued me. Rhys, the pixies, the uncertain new future, Red and Sakura and Lavender—how did all these pieces fit together? *What is the right thing to do?*

It all made my scales crawl with that uneasy, unnerved feeling. And because I was so uncomfortable, when I smelled smoke farther up the mountain and sensed the presence of other dragons, I immediately feared the worst.

At first I feared the *literal* worst, which was that the ice dragon had returned for revenge. But that wasn't very realistic. As I flew closer, I realized that there were *two* dragons—two very alive, very large dragons, and the smoke I could smell wasn't from them, but from a campfire.

There's going to be some kind of fight, I thought instantly. I knew from my experience with the ice dragon and the knights how destructive such fights could be. And I was so tired of people dying on my mountain!

I gave up any idea of being cautious and flew straight for the smoke.

And actually, looking back, it's a little funny—but right from that moment, I assumed I'd take the side of the person with the campfire. That person, I assumed, was some small and helpless human. I felt certain they would need help. I suppose most dragons would have assumed the opposite, and flown to the aid of their own kind. But I do live alone, taking care of tiny things, so I suppose that role just comes naturally to me now.

In any case, what I mean is, I wasn't looking at the other dragons at first. I was just looking at the ground. The evergreens gave way to a grassy clearing, and the smoke rose from a boulder sitting right in the middle of the grass. I came down very low, looking for anyone in trouble. When I recognized the man at the campfire, I was a little surprised.

"Hunter?" I called. He'd *told* me he wanted to gather flowers up on the mountain, but I hadn't really thought about what that meant. Just seeing him again was so confusing I sat right down in the grass.

"Ah, Daisy," he replied, turning to smile over his shoulder. He was so completely unflustered by my appearance, it made me want to laugh out loud. "I hope I didn't scare you. These seeds have to be roasted, otherwise they're poisonous. I thought I'd take care of it before—"

Two dark shadows passed over his head. They were large, and growing *enormous.* That meant only one thing: the unfamiliar dragons were coming in close.

Their speed left me with no choice. We could talk about seed roasting later. "Watch out!" I called to Hunter, before launching myself up over his head.

I'm actually not all that large, not for a dragon. But my unusual wings make me a little more agile than most, especially near the ground. I charged straight for the newcomers, flying up with the sun in my eyes. I didn't want to hit them—just to scare them, really. To make it clear that whoever they hoped to pick on had an ally. And to redirect their attention.

I collided with one and kept going up, reaching a safe distance before turning around. "Violence is not taken lightly on this mountain," I called down to them. My sight was still blurry from the sunlight, but I could tell by the sound of their wings they were both hovering above the forest, looking up at me. "If you have a quarrel to pick, you can settle it with *me*."

"We have no quarrel," one called. "We've come to deliver judgment."

Her tone did not sit well with me. "On a simple stranger out in the woods?" I challenged, hoping that Hunter had been prudent enough to seek cover.

"We aren't here for—"

"Shining Gift of Earth and Light, Guardian of Gold-tree," interrupted the other.

"How do you know my name?" I dropped slightly in the air, struck once more by surprise. Then I realized I recognized that voice. "Mother?"

"Child," she called back, as my vision slowly cleared and I recognized *her* as the dragon I'd bumped into. "We aren't here about your friend. We came here to find *you*."

"But . . . why?"

"To deliver judgment," the first dragon, someone I did not

know, repeated. "For your part in the death of one of our own."

Fourteen

A Knight's Test

Rhys

Quite frankly, I would have been entirely content had I *never* encountered the stranger from Miss Sakura's café again for the rest of eternity.

However, as my luck would have it, he came and sought me out the next day at Lavender's Tavern.

I had, rather obstinately, put in a full day's work, despite still feeling the residual effects of the magical attack the day before. Miss Red had actually been kind enough to order me some healing herbal salves from the local Witch, Trent, so I was no longer *quite* as stiff. Nonetheless, I will admit I sat with less grace than usual at my stool at the bar.

When *he* came up and claimed the stool next to mine, I sat

up straight.

"No harm meant, friend." Those were the first words he said to me, his hands held up in an amiable gesture. I am certain the look on my face was far less than amiable, but this only prompted him to chuckle at me. "I'm not here to talk about yesterday. Let us focus on the present. I have a gift for you—news, about Daisy."

I have absolutely no need for divine gifts. I may not be able to see my future or even solve my present problems, but I liked to think I had learned *that* lesson, at least. Accordingly, I turned back to my empty plate, staring ahead. "Thank you, but I do not need your news."

"What if *she* needs you to know?"

This sounded ominous, and I did not appreciate it. I glanced back at him suspiciously. Of course, he ignored me by focusing on Mme Lavender and ordering himself a drink.

He gestured to me as if to say, *and you? What are you drinking?* and Mme Lavender watched me with one eyebrow raised. I shook my head at her. The *last* thing I needed around this stranger was a clouded head.

"I was out on the mountain today," he said, once he had his mead in hand.

"I do not care to know your movements," I replied coldly.

"I saw two Elders from the Circle of Dragons stop by," he continued, as if I'd said nothing.

That was unexpected. I hesitated.

"I always thought Belville was safe. Even boring," the stranger mused, turning his gaze to the wooden ceiling above us, the lit hearths at each end of the room. "Who'd have thought *battles* were taking place here? Perhaps I should have started coming by sooner."

"I do not believe that measure would have *decreased* the number of battles," I observed through gritted teeth. I dearly wished to ask *why* he felt the need to tell me all this, but I also knew that he would never give me a direct answer.

At my rudeness, he set his glass upon the polished counter and considered me. I could feel his gaze sweep up and down, but I did my best not to show it. Finally he spoke, his voice cutting deftly through the noise. "You are something, aren't you, Sir Rowan? Or should I call you Rhys?"

"I would prefer you called me nothing at all."

"Oh, I wouldn't worry so much about a small thing like a name. But it is *difficult* to be someone new if you're clinging to an old title, isn't it?"

I recognized this as a question that was *not*, in fact, a question, and I allowed my grimace to tell him so.

The stranger laughed again. "You ought to be pleased with me, I think. I'm here with an opportunity for you."

"Why?" The tone of his voice had strayed into *dangerous* again. Any squire ought to know better than to accept a boon of any kind from a stranger like this.

"Let's just say it's a bit of kindred spirit."

"If your idea of 'kindred' has anything to do with Miss Daisy—"

"It doesn't. Rest assured." He leaned in, and I couldn't help it. I met his eyes. That green, the color of the hearts of fern, was suddenly deep and *far* too knowing. "You could say I'm a longstanding admirer of your mother's work. I'm . . . appreciative."

Appreciative. My mouth went dry. Only one kind of person *appreciates* the work of a trickster deity, and that's another trickster.

"Some tricks are for the greater good, Rhys," the stranger said with a smile. "Someone like you should see the value of perspective."

I wasn't sure what he meant, *the value of perspective, someone like me.* But it didn't matter; my throat was still far too dry for me to speak.

"Listen very carefully, because I will only put it this simply once," he continued. "It is time for someone to answer for the death of that ice dragon. The dragon council may move slowly, but nothing will prevent them from reaching a decision. Not even the truth will save your Daisy."

Not even the truth.

I killed the ice dragon. She didn't want to. She made me promise not to.

But if I reveal to a council of dragons that she had such close dealings with me, a knight, a sworn enemy . . . would it only make her situation worse?

The horror of it, I am certain, showed plainly in my eyes. He already knew. He might as well have read my thoughts.

"The trial is in three days' time," he said quietly. "Just a few days before the solstice. It is time to show her, Sir Rowan Grendale of the Tipped Ewer, what kind of knight you truly are."

Fifteen

Rules of the Job

Daisy

I don't think I made a very good first impression.

Well, my mother knows me, of course. I think, in retrospect, she figured out pretty quickly what was going on. Thank goodness *she* was the one I bumped into! I don't think the other judge, a volcanic dragon named Pele, would have been as kind about it. I tried explaining that I really did think that they were intruders . . . I mean, really, the ice dragon's death was more than a year ago. Could I really be expected to be *still* on the lookout for judgment?

According to the other dragons, yes.

"Being here alone with the pixies has damaged your sense of time," my mother told me, the morning after they arrived. After finding a place for themselves to stay higher on the mountain, she and Pele had settled in to "observe" for a few days before passing judgment. This made me even more uncomfortable than a trial, I think. While Pele was out surveying the mountain, my mother and I sat by the pixies' waterfall.

"I knew *something* was coming," I confessed. By that point I was feeling so melancholy about the whole thing that the pixies didn't even bother trying to play with me. They gave me and my mother a wide berth. "I just wasn't sure this would be it."

"Of course not. How would you know anything of dragon politics or trials, living way out here?" Mother glanced around at the rushing water, sparkling wet rocks, and riotous colorful wildflowers of our hideaway. "Has it always been so lush?"

"I like gardening," I said, still sounding utterly miserable. In a way, I was. Mother's reappearance with a massive, rocky red dragon like Pele had only reminded me how very *un*like a dragon I am sometimes.

"You like gardening?" Mother repeated, amused.

"In human form usually. It's easier that way. The plants here are easy to grow anyway, since they're so near the Tree," I explained. If I'd been in human form at that moment, I would've been blushing. "The pixies help me. They like growing all sorts of flowers."

My mother cocked her head, her burnished white scales glinting in the sunlight. "Is it this habit of gardening that got you involved with the knights in the first place, then?"

At first I said nothing. Mother and Pele had already heard my complete explanation of the ice dragon affair. Well, maybe not *totally* complete—I'd made it sound like Rhys and I were just . . . allies in battle, for a short time. I hadn't really thought that this would satisfy Mother, but I didn't want to drag Rhys into the trial. He is a good knight and very strong, but Pele was terrifying even to me, and anyway a knight at the mercy of dragons' judgment is unlikely to get a fair trial.

"I've been wondering," Mother continued quietly, "*how* you ended up out on the mountain alone, Daisy."

"I—I was doing work for Lavender," I admitted. "She runs the inn in town. Sometimes I do—did—the gardening at the little outpost she keeps—the tower Pele's gone to see. That's where the knights stayed, like I told you yesterday. But none of this is Lavender's fault."

"Of course," Mother said again. "So, if you were there before the ice dragon was summoned, gardening, in human form . . . you had a chance to speak to the knights?"

My head sank very, very low, until my nose was pressed into the moss and ferns beneath the boulder I was sitting on. There was a pixie hiding there, amongst the fiddleheads. I wasn't surprised—pixies love to spy. It's part of why they always have so much trouble amongst themselves. I felt kindly toward the little one, actually, and in that moment of relief I thought, *Is this the example I want to set for them?*

And then, *What do I really have to feel miserable and ashamed about, anyway?*

"Well . . . yes, actually, I did," I said, lifting my head. "And I learned a lot. Some of them were just as bad as the stories say. But they weren't *all* bad. And in the end, all the ones who meant to kill the ice dragon were killed first. But it's made me wonder ever since if, maybe, the pixies don't need me after all. Especially since they've made peace with the other pixies they were hiding from."

"Peace or no, I doubt the pixies would have fought off an ice dragon on the mountain," my mother observed wryly.

"Well, no. But that was only once. Surely you noticed it too," I said, turning more fully toward her. "You were guardian here once, and nothing happened. Did it?"

"Nothing notable enough to draw the attention of the Circle," Mother agreed.

"I just wonder if—if even the big, dangerous things that happen—they sort of work themselves out. Without a guardian. I mean, the ice dragon was so injured he could barely fly, after his fight with the knights. My part in the fight was very small."

"Then why involve yourself at all?"

"Well . . ." I sighed. There wasn't much use in being coy, I decided. The gossip had probably spread already anyway. "He wouldn't deal peacefully with me. He thought I was a traitor."

My mother, apparently, had decided not to make this easy. "Because of your duties with the pixies?"

"Because I didn't let him kill one of the knights," I said finally. The fear rose in my throat again—I wanted so badly for Rhys not to be part of this new danger—but realistically, I knew he was already in it. And there wasn't much point in continuing to be miserable.

"Why didn't you, Daisy?" Mother asked, leaning in. "Don't you think it might have made things simpler?"

A cloud passed over the sun, and away again. In the renewed sunlight, it was like I was seeing my mother differently. *That's exactly what she would have done,* I thought. *She was always a very strict and orderly guardian, up until the moment she decided she would leave.*

Should *I* have done that?

The question wasn't even tenable. Of *course* I should have saved Rhys.

The pixies at the other end of the grotto started trilling,

probably excited over some new butterfly or flower they'd found. They'd always been just as thrilled with Rhys. It had never mattered to them that he was a knight. All that mattered was that he was kind.

I sat up straighter. "I *don't* think it would have made anything simpler," I told my mother. "I think it's the Circle and all the centuries of—of prejudice that make things complicated. What could be more simple than the fact that I saved someone's life, because they needed help? It is not my fault that the ice dragon was so angry. It is not my fault he wouldn't reason. I know he had suffered, but he *caused* suffering, too. In the end, I only did my best. Not just what was best for the pixies, but what was best for all of the mountain, and—and best for *me*, too."

A twig snapped and as one, my mother and I turned. She sat up, turquoise wings flared out, teeth flashing. The *proper* guardian response.

But I only watched in mute horror as, amid a swarm of fluttering pixies, Rhys emerged from between the rocks.

Sixteen

No Verdict Wanted

Rhys

"Please let me be the one to atone." My first words to my lady, after weeks of loneliness.

It was not at all how I'd hoped a meeting with her might proceed. The incessant flap of pixie wings filled my ears, and between the excitable little creatures and the glare from the other dragon's scales, I could hardly see. Additionally, I had skipped breakfast that morning to ride up immediately, and in my haste to approach—augmented by the confusion a cloud of pixies inevitably causes—I'd managed to submerge one boot in the icy pool. In consequence my stomach was growling and I most likely smelled of soggy leather, two facts which I'm sure astute dragons could not help but notice.

I also hadn't intended to intrude on a private conversation . . . But I realized my mistake too late.

My lady said nothing.

"Why should you be the one to atone?" the unfamiliar dragon asked pointedly. I say 'unfamiliar,' but of course I noticed that the dragon's coloring and wing structure—so unusual as to be almost one-of-a-kind—echoed Daisy's. Undoubtedly this was a familial relation. Dimly I recalled my lady saying that her mother had joined the dragon's council.

I did my best to stand properly, presentably. Difficult when one is on a slippery rock and *still* surrounded by curious pixies. "Begging your pardon, madame. *I* am the one who struck the killing blow on the ice dragon in question."

At last Daisy moved; but her mother spoke first. "You? A knight?"

So they knew that much of the story, then, that a knight had been present. I was taken aback nonetheless. Glancing at myself, I realized that I was in fact wearing the shirt and trousers I often wore for work at Red's Alchemy and Potions—I'd been too hurried in the morning to put on full armor. And since my confrontation at the Pomegranate, I'd sworn off carrying my sword. In short, there was nothing on my person to indicate my former profession.

For a moment, I must admit I felt incredibly exposed.

My lady saved me, in her grace. "Mother," she said gently, rising, "this is Sir Rowan. As he says, he was present. But it is not," she added, with a very careful look in my direction, "necessary to bring him into the trial. You and Pele already know everything you need to know."

So that *is her wish. That,* at least, was entirely unsurprising. I had known to expect this from my lady. But that did not mean

I could stand aside in such a serious matter.

"Sir Rowan." Daisy's mother relaxed slightly, dropping down from 'could attack at any moment' to 'might attack later.' Such poses are frequently memorized by pages. In fact, I felt very much like a page as she continued staring at me. "I have indeed heard about you. But not, I think, as much as I should have."

"There is no more to say," my lady protested, her fervor such that she actually positioned herself between her mother and me. "Sir Rowan is not involved in the trial. Everything about him is entirely *separate* from the trial. Besides, you have no authority over him."

I can not describe how it stung each time my lady said *Sir Rowan.* "On the contrary," I declared, "There can be no inquiry into who killed the ice dragon without *me* present."

"My daughter is right," said Daisy's mother, rather unexpectedly.

"But as I have said before, *I*—"

"Sir Rowan, please, stop—"

"—was the one who—"

"—you don't know what is at stake—"

"You will have no part of the trial," Daisy's mother announced, rising up again to stare over her daughter at me. Her voice, literally above the arguments of myself and my lady, demanded instant silence. "Sir Rowan, as I have already told you, my daughter is right. This trial is not about who killed the ice dragon. We have known for some time that it was *you.* That matter was deemed a side effect of the true issue at stake."

I nearly slipped into the water again. I began to wonder if that terrible stranger had set me up. "What," I managed finally, hoarsely, "is the issue at stake, may I ask?"

"Our trial concerns Daisy's execution of her duties as

guardian, and whether she abused that role during her part in the deceased dragon's demise," was the grave answer.

My lady was silent.

"You can not," I said, without fully meaning to. "If *I* am outside your jurisdiction, then certainly my lady's own arrangement with the pixies must be. They have never had any complaint to make of her—nor *could* they. She has only ever been upstanding, thorough, considerate, and deeply kind in her role as guardian. There is no doubt in my mind that the pixies feel this also. Therefore, if they are satisfied, then what right has a separate council of judging her, when they know nothing of her duty and her daily concerns?"

The pixies around me started cheering. I had forgotten they were there. They had given up flying around me and instead had perched on my head and on my shoulders, pulling at fabric and tousling my hair, but this inconvenience was forgiven in light of the fact that *they agreed with me.*

We were, however, only so many tiny voices against one very large one. Daisy's mother rose up again, spreading her wings. "You forget, *knight,* that I was once guardian here too."

"That may be, but at present you are *not,*" I said hotly. I was not to be cowed. "By my understanding, it has been more than a century since you relinquished your post. Such an era is nothing to a dragon, or even to a pixie, I will concede. But that does not hold for the world beyond you. The simple fact is that times have changed. The mountain, the town, the rumors, and yes—the knights. They have changed. Your understanding has not."

"*Rhys,*" my lady interrupted. "You can't just say things like that!"

I did not care if she was abashed. Just hearing her say my

name made my heart sing. "I will tell the truth to any who will listen."

"Did you come here to pick a fight?" My lady's tone was exasperated.

I must admit, the similarity to what William had said to me a few days before did strike a chord. But I was unmoved. The pixies agreed with me, and I would not see Daisy unfairly treated. "If my options are to stand and fight or to watch wrongdoing, then I stand."

"Nobody told you to be here watching," my lady protested.

"I came here to accept the blame that ought to be laid at my door," I replied. "Even if you will not allow me that much, you must at least understand that I can not see *more* blame laid at yours."

"Daisy," her mother interrupted before she could speak. "It is clear to me that this conversation has run its course. I am going to join Pele in the investigation of the ruins. I suggest you explain to your knight what his other options are."

She did not address me directly, but she did look in my direction. While I did not feel that I agreed with her in any detail, she did still demand respect. I bowed as she left.

The pixies swarmed around me again, dislodged by the movement. To be honest, I paid neither them nor the wingbeats of the retreating dragon any mind.

Your knight. It was the one usage of the word which I found I did not mind.

Seventeen

Correctly Ever After

Daisy

As I watched my mother leave, the confusion and frustration I felt faded a little.

In their place . . . there was Rhys.

"You shouldn't be here," I hissed. It was so annoying, how perfectly he spoke, and how the pixies had somehow chosen *his* side. He wasn't even supposed to have a side in this! It wasn't supposed to be an argument!

And it didn't help that I wanted so badly to transform. But talking to him face-to-face would only result in more complications, especially because the pixie charm that allows me to change forms doesn't actually include *clothing* as part of its magic.

Pixies, as I may have noted before, aren't exactly known for their practicality.

"I *should* be here," Rhys insisted, still standing firm. Still half-covered by little winged forms.

There was a moment of electric silence before he seemed to realize what he'd said. Then he cleared his throat and added, "What I mean is, I should be part of the trial, my lady. Even if it has nothing to do with the ice dragon fight. Surely my role as the pixies' guide—"

"It isn't *your* role that's in question," I said quickly, surprised by the bitterness in my own voice.

"Perhaps it should be, then. Perhaps if I had—"

"Rhys, the answer to this problem is not to add *more!* It's not going to help anything, dragging *you* into all of this too!"

"Then what, pray tell, *is* the answer?"

"It—it is—the answer is just to let Mother and Pele do as they see fit," I said, trying to squish much more confidence into my words than I felt. "They're the ones with the authority here. It's not like they're ill-meaning—"

"Forgive me, but I would not abide any authority on this matter nor, in fact, on this mountain other than *yours,*" Rhys interrupted.

I ignored the warmth that flooded my chest at hearing this. "Can't you see that's exactly the problem? I have no idea what I'm doing. Not really. These are serious matters, Rhys. Somebody *died*—*several* somebodies died—and it was on my watch!"

I expected this to be the last word, but he was quick—so quick—with an answer.

"Did any *pixies* die, my lady?"

"N-no . . . But it's not enough! You know that isn't enough.

It is *our* mountain, the pixies' mountain, and we never wanted that kind of strife here."

"My lady, I have told you repeatedly, it is *not your fault* that others came seeking you and the Tree—"

"—but isn't that exactly the situation I'm supposed to be here to handle?"

"And did you not?"

Rhys and I were staring at each other. The pixies had gone so still they looked like little carvings, little knickknacks, pinned all over his shirt. His *shirt*—it was so sweet to see him without armor on—so tender to think that he had come all the way here and had brought no defense, yet he wanted to defend *me,* of all people, after everything I'd done . . .

"Miss Sakura insists," said Rhys very quietly, very steadily, "that I err in never speaking my mind. Well, I will tell you what I think. I think you have done everything the very best guardian could do. You have fulfilled each and every one of your *actual* responsibilities. But you have no pride in your efforts. Why? Because you are *holding yourself to another standard.* You expect things of yourself that no one else has expressed. You have cleared one hurdle, but you insist you should have cleared three.

"*I* think you *want* to be on trial," he continued, blue eyes sharp and burning. "You insist on feeling guilty. You have *carried* this guilt with you, for years, despite everything I have tried to say. So now you surrender yourself without a fight."

"It was fighting that caused this trouble in the first place," I mumbled. But it was a weak protest.

"Not all fighting involves swords," Rhys said firmly. "You don't have to let their judgment control you. You don't have to acquiesce."

"Rhys, they haven't even made their judgment yet."

"But you have already decided what their outcome should be, have you not? If you hadn't . . . then why would you wish to protect myself and any others from taking part in the trial?"

"That isn't it," I insisted, though now that he said it, it really felt like that *might* be it. Or part of it. But I knew at least one other part of the problem to be true. "I just don't want you injured. That's all. Not ever, and especially not because *I* wasn't strong enough to do my duty correctly."

"Correctly?" Rhys shook his head. "Daisy, there *is* no 'correctly.' If you focus too closely on what is *right,* then you will forget what is in front of you. It took a severe blow to the head for me to find that out. You don't have to find out so violently. You don't have to do this, not alone. Who told you that you have done anything wrong?"

I knew the answer. *No one.* He was right, about more things than I wanted to admit.

I rose up, distancing myself. "The whole point of a trial is finding out the correct thing. You just have to make sure you're nowhere near it when it happens."

"You still refuse any help?"

There was something—something I wasn't sure I'd ever heard before in Rhys's voice. I faltered, trying to pinpoint it.

Then I remembered the look on Hunter's face at the Pomegranate Café. *I made that mistake once,* he'd said. *I won't make it again.*

"This doesn't concern you," I told Rhys. "It isn't a question of help. It's just a question of doing what's right. The right thing is for you to stay out of it, in Belville."

Rhys had already turned and was walking away when, quietly, I added the last part. The truest part. "Stay safe."

Eighteen

Friendly Advice

Rhys

It isn't a question of help.

Apparently, it was not a matter for thinking through with any kind of perspective, either. And let me be clear—I'm referring to *myself*, not my lady. To say that she was being stubborn and almost infuriatingly selfless is as useless as saying the sky is blue. Such had always been Daisy's faults. They are common enough in anyone who has been raised or trained to protect someone else. I knew that well, myself.

No, it was not her manner that upset me; it was that I could not reach her. I did not know *how*. I tried sharing my thoughts with her, but even that I did poorly, only sharing half of what I should have.

I didn't tell her that I loved her.

By the time I came to regret that fact, though, I was halfway down the mountain and it was too late to turn around. To turn back at that point, to show up at the pixies' grotto again, would have indicated a lack of faith in my lady. That was the farthest thing possible from the truth. I knew absolutely that Daisy could overcome any trial she faced. She didn't need my help.

But she did *deserve* it.

"How do I manage to make things worse and worse?" I asked Nessie, my horse.

Nessie snorted, his head bobbing among the heavily laden branches of oak and fir.

"And why," I wondered, mostly to myself, "is it so very difficult to learn *how* to help?"

Neither Nessie nor the forest had an answer.

I did not hurry back to town; I had no need to. By the time I returned to Lavender's tavern, the sun had all but disappeared below the western horizon. I retreated to my room without speaking to anyone. Given my track record with words, it didn't seem worth the risk.

My mood was not improved after a restless night. My dreams had been filled with Daisy, and yet I woke often, seeing her but never reaching her. Generally speaking I am not one to be lazy, but by the time the sun rose again in the east, I was inclined to give up entirely.

By mid-morning I might have even dozed off again, lost in half-won dreams, but for a knock that sounded on the door.

"Rhys!" called a familiar voice—William. "We're coming in."

We?

The term couldn't possibly include Daisy. She would be busy, up on the mountain with the dragons and the pixies; and I doubted she'd ever want to talk to me again, anyway. All the same, I made an effort to sit up.

We apparently meant William, Miss Sakura, and Mister Luca, who spilled into the room like so many toy boats down a fast-moving creek. An odd grouping of people that did nothing to shake the confusion that lingered from my dreams. At least they shut the door behind them.

"You don't look very well," Miss Sakura said. Normal, genteel people might have considered saying 'good morning,' but shadow witches, I've often observed, are not strong on polite observances. I was simply grateful she hadn't brought her accursed stranger with her.

And—to be honest—she may well have had a point. Her words reminded me to think of appearances. The quilted blanket was on the floor, the bedsheets twisted around my legs, and it seemed I had never actually undressed from the day before. No doubt my hair was shockingly rumpled and my face sallow, too. For once, though, I really couldn't bring myself to care.

"We brought you breakfast," Mister Luca said unnecessarily. In his arms he carried a large tray laden with tea pot, cups, and mounds of quiches and pastries. "Red said you've been doing so well lately, eating full meals, you know, and she didn't think you should stop. She says hello, by the way. She would have come herself, but she didn't think leaving *me* to watch the potions shop would have been any good, and Frank—that's my assistant, I think you've met—anyway, Frank will only ever watch the bookshop. Plus Red was expecting some orders to come in, and she has to finish up the sparkle potions for the Litha party at the café."

Ah, the Pomegranate. Mention of the party made me look at

Miss Sakura again. I found it difficult to believe or care that there would still be a Litha.

William hopped up onto the bed beside me. No doubt Mme Lavender would hate to think of animals—even magical ones—on her furniture, but I must admit I appreciated the gesture. I even leaned into him, slightly, as Miss Sakura pulled over a chair and Mister Luca claimed the blanket on the floor. The tray went on to the bedside table, from which Miss Sakura began pouring cups and filling plates for everyone present.

So this isn't to be a quick visit.

Miss Sakura handed me my plate with a particularly pointed look, and it occurred to me that I'd never replied to Mister Luca's kindness. With an effort, I said at last, "I appreciate Miss Red's concern. However . . . how, may I ask, did you know . . ."

"You mean, 'however did anyone manage to see me ride into town like a thundercloud on my massive blue horse last night,' and 'oh, but I thought I did such a sneaky job of clomping up the stairs to my room in front of a roomful of diners'?" Miss Sakura sipped primly at her tea. "Word got 'round."

I frowned, mostly at my own reflection in my cup.

"You went up to talk to her, then?" William asked. "Hunter came by yesterday and said—"

"Please," I interrupted. "If I *never* hear another word from him again, it will be too soon."

William went quiet, and it occurred to me that my vehemence had been misplaced. But though I was afraid I'd hurt my friend, I could not think what to do about it.

"He didn't tell anyone what it was all about," Miss Sakura said, picking up where William had left off blithely, as though discussing the weather. "By the way, Glacial gave us those stuffed rolls specifically for you, so you're going to have to eat all of them. If I were you, I'd start now."

The non sequitur was somehow even more annoying than her relevant remark. I stared at the shadow witch for a moment, failed to find any words, and instead dropped my gaze to Mister Luca. The safe presence in the room.

"I know it's all a bit much," he said, with a smile that was welcome for its softness. "I was used to living alone too, once, remember. But we mean well. Red was really worried about you, and so was William, and you know *that* is saying something."

"And Sakura just invited herself along," Miss Sakura added, wryly continuing Mister Luca's explanations for him. More soberly, she added, "Actually, Sir Rowan, I—it's been pointed out to me that I owe you an apology. I haven't been easy on you. In fact at first I was annoyed because I figured that anyone who's been around as long as you have should have sorted out all his—his *nonsense* by now. But that's not totally fair. Because you *do* have a very good grip on things when it's just you, don't you? It's just your relationship with Daisy that has you thrown off, and I can't expect you to have any experience dealing with that, because relationships like what you two have built are a very rare thing."

I set my plate to one side. "A very well-spoken apology, Miss Sakura. Would that I could accept it. You see, you have perhaps erred in the other direction . . . and given me too much credit. I am 'thrown off,' as you put it, by my relationship with Miss Daisy. That is true. But I find . . . now that I am forced to take a closer look at my life and my behavior . . . that I have not been at all responsible with my other relationships, either."

I glanced down at William, who lay beside me as I spoke. He shook his black ears, looking over the edge of the bed as he said, "It's alright. We all know this has been difficult for you."

After the briefest hesitation, I laid my hand on his fur. This time when he looked up I could see the smile in his eyes that said, *all is forgiven.*

"You are all," I said quietly, "much, much too good for the likes of me."

"Yes, and so is Daisy," Miss Sakura said airily. But she, too, smiled as she added, "Although apparently she isn't too clear-sighted about relationships either."

My mouth opened—normally, my impulse would be to defend my lady—and then closed. Miss Sakura was right. Of course. And one glance at Mister Luca's kind smile beside her reminded me that no offense was meant.

"Not very many people are," the scholar said gently. "That's why we're here."

I glanced back down at the rolls on my plate and, this time, took one. As I ate, I explained the situation to the others. All of it. I tried to be as succinct as I could, but by the time I was finished, most of the pastries were gone and Miss Sakura had used her magic to reheat the tea twice.

"Do you think she's in real danger?" Mister Luca asked when I was done.

"I couldn't say for certain. I am unfamiliar with dragon law. I do believe, however, that Daisy is strong enough to stand for herself," I said, watching the last of the tea swirl in my cup.

"And as you yourself pointed out, we don't actually know what their decision will be," Miss Sakura broke in, brisk. "It could very well be that this whole thing is a formality, and they don't really intend to punish her at all."

"But there's something else," William rumbled. "It isn't the trial that's bothering you."

I had to agree. "No, it isn't. Not exactly. What bothers me is that she thinks she, and she alone, deserves punishment. And I don't know what to do to help her. I don't know how to express . . . everything."

"Well, first things first," said Miss Sakura. "We can all agree that, despite certain overt differences, you and Daisy are very alike. Right? You both spend most of your time thinking about how you 'must be strong and protect someone else,' and all that kind of thing."

All that kind of thing. Not the most respectful way I've heard knighthood described, but then, I wasn't exactly a knight anyway. I sighed. "In essence, yes."

Miss Sakura took the last elderflower fritter from the tray, looking rather pleased with herself. "So. What has helped *you?*"

Wide-eyed, I glanced between Luca, William, and Sakura herself. "Why . . . you three, and Red, and Glacial. You all have."

"Whether you wanted us to or not," William observed with good humor.

"What specifically about us?" Luca asked the question, since Sakura had her mouth full.

I considered him. I was aware that, in my own mind, I'd given up using titles when thinking of them. After sharing my story with them, sharing how many meals with them?—after everything, they were not strangers. *My friends.*

"Not speaking," I said slowly as the realization sank in. Sakura tilted her head, and I told her, "You accused me of not speaking my mind. It stuck with me, because you were right. I—I tried telling everything to Miss Daisy, though I left the most important parts out. And it didn't help. Because what has truly helped *me* was not when you were speaking. It was when you listened to me."

"Huh." Sakura polished off her donut, grinning. "I have to admit, I didn't think of it myself. But it sounds like you're on to something."

"So what will you do?" Luca asked, leaning forward.

"She told me she wants to stand trial alone," I mused. "That is, regretfully, the one thing I really gave her the chance to say. So I will respect that. However . . . afterward . . ."

William stirred beside me. "Afterward, you better go see if she'll talk to you. Because if you don't and you keep being mopey at the shop, Red will probably try to do it *for* you."

Nineteen

A Dragon's Trial

Daisy

Dragons will live and live and go on living until someone else kills them. It's very, very rare for one to die of disease, and even rarer for one to die of old age. So even though they're generally considered big and scary and even monstrous by most other people, you'd think they'd end up being quite philosophical, right?

And you'd think a bunch of philosophical beings would devise some kind of elaborate trial system relying on testimony from all sides and long speeches and concerns about *truth*, right?

Well, that's what I thought. I mean, there was always an outside chance that Pele might get frustrated and breathe fire, or something—that's why I didn't want anyone flammable to come—not to be mean to Pele, of course, but she was the dragon I knew least about. And I definitely saw her nostrils smoking as she tried to talk to the pixies. (That delighted them, unfortunately. They've never seen anyone breathe fire—I can only breathe a sort of poisonous, paralyzing mist.)

But for a trial that was just trying to determine what the parameters of my role as guardian really *were,* and if I'd ever abused them, I figured we'd mostly be talking about the pixies' history and the dragons' worries about encroaching on each others' territory, or something. Not that any other dragons live near Belville, but clearly they would want to pass through from time to time—or they might show up by accident, like the ice dragon. And of course no one wanted the immediate answer in that case to be *death.*

Anyway, I flew up to the very tippy-top of Belville Mountain before the sun had even risen on the day of the trial, and sitting there on the rocks at daybreak, I discovered that I'd been wrong.

Apparently, my trial was to be a *test of strength.*

All I remember about that moment is looking down, so far down, past the trees and the sliver of the pixies' waterfall, all the way down to where the town was nestled in the mountain's shadow. And I thought, *Is Rhys safe?*

And then I thought, *of course he isn't.*

Because we're both the same.

After that I didn't think for a long time, because Pele knocked me off the mountain with one incredible sweep of her tail.

I guess "test of strength" means "fight."

My mother sat atop the boulders, watching, performing her duty as Impartial Observer, or whatever they called it. So it was a sort of one-on-one duel, I suppose. But I never was any match for Pele. If I am larger than a café when in dragon form, she is larger than a tavern. In the past two days, I'd found out that she *was* in fact a volcano dragon, and a very ancient one at that. Her scales were hard as rocks and her breath was so hot even I could hardly stand it, and that was just her *breath.* She definitely could breathe fire. In fact, I saw that pretty quickly, as she set the trees alight when I didn't get up immediately after being swatted down the mountainside.

I flew up into the air. There wasn't anywhere else to hide. Someone like Rhys or Sakura, someone who is smart, would have thought of strategy—they might have told me to use my speed and try to wear her out, maybe. But those ideas never occurred to me. My idea of "fighting" tends to be a bit more free-form, you might say.

I did dodge when she rushed at me, though. Her nails glinted dark gold in the rising sun, and they were wicked sharp. At the last minute my self-preservation kicked in, and I dove to one side to avoid her touching me. I was able to right myself and turn pretty quickly, but so was Pele. She went up, and up, never losing her momentum, and then she curved through the air and came back for me, this time coming down out of the sky.

Good thing the sun wasn't fully up. I dodged her again, this time more easily. I went to one side again, and she kept going down. She was so very big, but she was powerful enough to keep herself from going *straight* into the ground. Still, she did knock over a few of the tallest trees, and she paused midair, probably confused because of the sudden rush of having to change direction.

I saw my chance.

Still not for fighting back, though—like I said, I'm pretty

bad at duels. I'd do anything for the pixies, of course, and I've never actually *lost* a fight for them, but my actions have always been—well, the kind word for it might be *instinctual,* rather than trained. So in that moment I didn't do anything tactical. Actually what I did was pick up a boulder and use it to squash some of the fire that was going down the mountainside.

Just because I was on trial didn't mean the forest needed to burn.

I'm not sure what exactly about this made Pele angry, but *something* did. She roared, so loud the earth beneath us shook. Again she charged right at me, but I was stuck between the forest on one side and the burning shrubs on the other, so I couldn't dodge to the side. I went up. I was pretty proud of myself actually. It felt like I was finally making use of my agility. But I think Pele must have known what I would do, because as she passed under me she caught hold of my tail.

At first it felt like a horrible rush in my stomach, like the world had flip-flopped. Then after a moment of pulling me along, she threw me into the mountain.

I am good at stopping in place, though. It's something else my wing structure is suited for, that most other dragons do not expect, I think. But I do it with the pixies all the time—they like to play tag. Plus they think it is funny when the wind changes because of my wings.

At that moment in the fight, my head was still spinning, but the thing about Pele's claws being so hard and so *hot* was that they were very noticeable. So the moment she let go of me, I realized I was free, and part of me—that part which, I suppose, had been in training with the pixies for years—instantly said, *stop.* And I did. At first I just felt like I was hovering in a vacuum, but as my senses came back, I realized slowly that I was inches from the cliffside. She'd tried to throw me straight into the mountain. In fact, with each wing beat, dust and pebbles rained down behind me.

Pele roared again.

She charged again and this time I had room, so I went down.

And then, since I had a free moment as she was trying to maneuver around the cliff, I put out another section of the fire.

I wasn't thinking anything in particular. It was all happening too fast. But Pele had settled on top of the cliff and when I turned I saw she was staring at me, and I knew *she* was thinking, even though I had no idea what her thoughts might be.

Her thoughts became clear, though, when she launched off of the cliff and didn't come at me.

Instead, she flew down the mountain, toward the pixies' grotto.

No. That was the only thing I could think, but I thought it with every fiber of my being. I might have cried out, even, but all I could hear was the whistling of wind in my ears.

Pele must have known I was following her. She flew faster, and faster. I am agile but I couldn't match her speed. I didn't have her momentum. She was so much bigger than me, and so much heavier, and we were going down, down, skimming over the trees, and in a minute she would be there, and even though I'd told everyone to stay safe inside and they were magically protected I'd just seen the earth literally shake when Pele roared and there was no telling what she could do to the mountain around them especially now that she had such velocity behind her and I'd made her so angry and we'd be there in the very next breath and—

I hurtled myself at Pele with everything I could muster. I latched on to her side, which was a mistake, because instantly her claws were digging into my scales, breaking them. But I kept going. I forced her to go down into the trees to one side of the grotto. We crashed through the old growth like so many matchsticks. I registered pain, but we weren't far enough away yet. I kept pushing her until we'd rolled off a nearby cliff and crashed into a meadow.

Pele had the upper hand, always. She might have been surprised but really, this was what she had wanted all along, and I knew it. She rolled so I was flat on the ground and then she reared up, and I knew without even thinking that *this is it.*

But I couldn't fly.

I couldn't even lift myself up.

One of the trees must have gone straight through my wing.

But this is home. This is my home. It's my home on the line . . .

Twenty

Kitchen Ghosts

Rhys

When we heard the roaring in Belville, everything stopped.

It was well before business hours, but ever since William, Luca, and Sakura had talked some sense into me, I'd found I had more energy. I was up and tending to Nessie in the stable behind the tavern when I first heard it.

Or rather, I should say I *felt* it. The ground itself was rumbling, as though an earthquake had struck.

Indeed, some fools believed it *was* only an earthquake. It was too early yet for any business at Lavender's, but as I crossed the Square to the Pomegranate Café, the gossip was already flying. The lights at Red's Alchemy & Potions were out, but I could see William's face in the window upstairs. In the streets, farmers hustled back to their farms, neglecting their deliveries. A group of voyeurs clustered on the Pomegranate's front patio, craning their necks in any direction for signs of a catastrophe.

I went straight into the café, expecting perhaps to run into its owner, the shadow witch. Surely *she* would know something of this—something more than what I feared.

Instead, it was Miss Glacial I found behind the counter.

"I only just got in myself," she said, wiping her hands on a vibrantly pink apron as she sidled from foot to foot. "Saki hates early mornings. Usually we only have a few regulars, and I don't mind taking care of their orders. This is the best time for baking. *Baking*," she repeated, apparently to herself. "That is why I am here. I was putting the cinnamon rolls in the oven. They'd nearly risen, and I was mixing the icing, and there's the muffins to do next . . ."

"Miss Glacial," I said gravely. The little baker jumped and refocused on the cash register before looking up at me. "I wonder if you are busy?"

"Me? No. I'm not busy. I'd like to be busy," she rambled. Her white tail swished behind her.

"I, also, would like to be busy," I confessed. "Perhaps you could use some help in the kitchen."

"I—I—I could," Miss Glacial decided eventually. "No one will come out right now. And then everyone will be out. We'll need lots of food. I need to be *baking* . . ."

With what was already a familiar refrain, she shut her register and gestured me to follow her towards the back of the café. I hadn't planned to spend time there, particularly not if Sakura wasn't present, but I found that this new plan suited me very well. In fact, I felt just as jumpy as Miss Glacial sounded.

A swinging door let us into the kitchen, which was small

but serviceable, and very well set up. A bank of counters and ovens lined the inner wall, while shelves and storage lined the outer, with a large sink and drying rack at the far end. At Miss Glacial's insistence, I donned a light blue apron and soon began work on raspberry muffin batter. When the second roar sounded, the pair of us only mixed and rolled and ladled and washed even harder.

Finding such occupation was a perfect solution for my nerves, but I'm afraid it couldn't distract me from the pain I felt when, ever so faintly, I heard Daisy cry out.

There was a distant crash and then silence for a long while. I could only hear my own heartbeat, and then a rushing which I realized was the tap I'd left running. I turned it off and dried my hands, leaving the rest of the pots in the sink where, thanks to my inattention, they would be able to soak.

"Do you—do you think it's over?" Miss Glacial asked quietly. She leaned against rather than sat upon a stool, which she had dragged to set opposite one of her ovens.

"I do not dare to think of it," I admitted in a whisper.

Morning light came in strong from the window above the sink, and the windowed door to the back patio. In its rays, flour and powdered sugar danced, giving the little kitchen an ethereal feel. There was no sound any more. There was only the warmth from the ovens, and the spicy sweet smell of cinnamon.

"Saki should be in soon. If she isn't already," Miss Glacial remarked. From her stool, she kept her gaze level on the window in her oven, where the last of the muffins baked.

"I confess I did come here thinking I might speak to her. But I am not certain I have the heart for it now," I said, settling against the wet counter behind me.

At this, in the stillness, Miss Glacial finally glanced my way.

"We . . . we don't ever get to be something else, do we. Not really."

The pain in her voice was something I had, in my selfishness, forgotten that other people could feel. I'd been too focused on my own feelings of loss and shame and confusion. But her words reminded me of our first conversation, when she'd so innocently insisted I could *be something else* than a knight. And now, looking at her, I noticed unshed tears in her mismatched eyes.

"You are a baker," I said softly.

"A baker who recognizes when dragons roar, and can think of nothing to do but hide from herself," she replied bitterly.

"A wounded baker is still a baker."

"Wounded," she echoed vaguely. "Yes. I guess that's the word for it. But I—I—my people are not dragons," she said suddenly, as though it had occurred to her she needed to explain herself. "Not exactly. But I know. I—I've traveled. I can tell what must be going on. On the mountain. I heard about the trial. I know that's it, and it's nothing to do with me. But it still scares me. I'm not like Daisy. I'm—I ran away. I did it all myself."

All the wounding, I surmised. It was an easy conclusion to draw. For all the mixed-up details in her half-told story, it was recognizable to me. When I'd first arrived in Belville I, too, had been wounded over and over by my own persistence in valuing duty above myself—even when that duty was long over and gone.

"You do not have to explain yourself," I said very clearly. "And you do not have to be like Miss Daisy. Not very many people are."

"No. Not very many people are strong," Miss Glacial whispered.

I frowned. Something in the way she said it, the fatalism in her voice, reminded me of William reprimanding me for picking a fight with a god in a coffee shop. And while William had been right, of course, I didn't think Miss Glacial was. In fact her statement helped me finally put words to a suspicion I'd had all along. "There comes a time when strength is not helpful. Even divine strength will fail. Why else would the gods be so unwilling to confront fate directly?"

Miss Glacial's mismatched eyes focused on me with alarm, but I was thinking of a time long ago, of a trickster deity and a stolen seed. *It would have been so much simpler to mediate an actual truce, or even just to tell someone what was going on.* Sakura would laugh at me for thinking such a thing, given how reticent I could be. But what a tangled web had been woven by those three "gifts!"

"Sometimes you find yourself beyond your limits," Miss Glacial said, unexpectedly. I looked up to see her alarm had faded into thoughtfulness. "Someone said that to me once. He said—they said—sometimes you give in. If you can. I think that's what you mean."

"A rather glib way of putting it," I observed, wringing out a dish towel. I had a feeling I knew who had told her that.

"Yes. You may be right. But you know what I just thought?" She shifted against her stool, becoming more animated. "You said 'wounded baker.' That's what I am. Maybe that's just *one* thing though. Maybe you can't change the things you've been, but you can be more than one thing. I think that's what Saki would say. I don't know what you would call yourself. But I would say . . . one thing you could say you are could be 'kind friend.'"

"You could say the same," I replied, when the tightness in my

114

throat had subsided and I could find words again.

Glacial smiled as she wiped at her nose with her shoulder, the muscles and scars of her bare arm a now-forgotten reminder of a martial past. "Well. Do you think—do you think she's okay?"

"I wish I knew. I almost rode up there this morning, when I first heard it," I confessed. "But she wanted to do this herself. I think if I had been there, it would only have made her worry. She—she wanted . . ."

"It was something she needed to do," Glacial offered, nodding. Prompted by some force entirely unknown to me, she leaned forward and pulled the last tray of muffins from the oven, and they came out perfectly—caught right in the moment of caramelization, just before burning. Sharp raspberry and sweet white chocolate vied with cinnamon in the quiet air. There were, I realized, new sounds in the café beyond: the hiss of steam, the scraping of chairs, a low murmur of voices. Sakura must have come in, and with her, the curiosity of the townsfolk.

"I know a little," Glacial continued once the muffins were settled on a rack. "About dragon law. I think you're right to let her decide. She'll be fine. But—she might need time to—recover."

The idea that Daisy had been hurt in the course of the trial was a lance through my stomach, but Glacial's words were only an acknowledgment of what I had feared from the very first roar. Dragons do not roar unless there is danger.

"I can bake you something," Glacial went on, hesitantly. "Something to help her feel better. To heal. You could take it to her. When it's time."

"Thank you." The words were so earnest, so big I could feel them catching in my throat. "I will do exactly that . . . when it is time."

Twenty-One

A New Role

Daisy

Only *some* dragons breathe fire. Some actually breathe ice, and some breathe disease, I've heard. It all depends on what kind of dragon it is, and where they come from. My family has a sort of paralysis attack—I've used it in the past to stop rabid animals. I actually used it on the ice dragon, too, though it only worked for a moment.

I did my best to use it on Pele . . .

. . . You can probably guess the results. No effect whatsoever.

Actually—that's not quite right. Pele had pinned me on the ground and I couldn't escape, so I did my best to use that attack right before her claws came down. She went right through the shiny cloud and kept on going. But she stopped just an inch away from my face, and there was a wheezing, creaking sound, like granite rubbed on granite.

She was laughing.

"Shining Gift of Earth and Light, Guardian of Gold-tree," she said, lifting herself up again, "The strength of your convictions holds. You and your actions are worthy."

I think I passed out.

Next thing I really remember is sitting above the grotto with my mother in human form. Dragons don't have much notion of *healing*, aside from retreating to a cave and sleeping for a hundred years until they feel better. As a human, though, there are so many helpful things you can do. All my cuts and scrapes were bandaged up, and the pixies had even brought me magical buds and leaves from the Tree, which helped speed the healing process. But the loss of one wing as a dragon manifested as a deep and terrible pain in my human shoulder, a pain even the life-sustaining magic of the Tree couldn't fix entirely.

"It'll come back," my mother assured me. She sat beside me, our bare legs dangling alongside the waterfall as we looked out over the garden. "But it will take time, even with the pixies looking after you. I wouldn't try changing back all summer, if I was you."

Of course I was grateful just to be alive, and to be well enough to see straight. But I do think I grimaced at that. The pixies mean well, but of us all, Rhys has always been the best healer. And how could I go to see him now? How could I apologize and explain things, and tell him what happened? If I showed up in town after *walking* down the mountain, they'd probably think I was some sort of forest banshee, all weak and wobbly and disheveled. I don't think I've ever walked so far in my life, except maybe with Rhys.

117

"You might have died, pulling a stunt like that," Pele observed. She crouched on the other side of the waterfall, still in dragon form. Her voice was loud and low.

"If it weren't for the Tree, you might still run that chance," Mother added. "Daisy, you must be more careful. We are creatures of the air, after all. Where would we be without our wings?"

"It wouldn't matter where I was if I'd failed the pixies," I said, my heels kicking at the mossy rock beneath us. "I still don't understand. Why did I pass the trial? I didn't win the fight. I wasn't strong enough."

Pele rumbled. "It was never about how physically strong you are, little one."

"And it's especially not about how strong you are compared to others," Mother agreed. "The trial was about your choices. And you chose to keep doing what you knew to be right, even at great cost to yourself."

"If you're the sort who will risk her well-being to head off a threat to those she loves, and who will keep fighting when she's all but beat—the sort you have *proven* you are," said Pele, "then the Circle trusts your dedication to your duty, and your judgment."

"The ice dragon," I murmured. "You believe it *was* necessary, then?"

"Yes. And it isn't just that, Daisy," my mother said. "You showed no predisposition to violence, so there is no need to think any peaceable visitor to this mountain would be in danger."

"Of course not," I protested. "I've been saying that all along. I didn't mean for anyone to die."

Pele made that laughing sound again. "Saying it is one thing, little one. A trial is for *proving* it."

The stress and terror of the morning hadn't passed yet, not enough so that I could join her in laughing. But as I looked out at the blue sky and the lush, unburned forest, and the rows of blooming flowers and the glimmer of wings where the pixies sat watching this strange and exciting meeting, I sighed. *It's over.*

"Mother," I said, unable to stop the question that rose to my lips, "why did you leave? Why did you *really* stop being guardian?"

She turned to me smiling, and ran her hand through my wild hair. "For exactly the same reason that you succeeded today, and that I *knew* you would succeed, daughter. You have always been kindhearted, and inside that kind heart, there has always burned the flame of pride. You take your kindness so very seriously, without even meaning to. Dear one, you were always going to be the very best guardian of us all. That is the real reason I left—to give you that chance. It was time. Time to give you the space to be what you needed to be."

"I—" I choked back tears, glancing around us at the pixies again. "But I don't know what I need to be. I have been worried I wasn't enough. Rhys said that's why I wanted to go on trial, and he was right."

"You *do* know," my mother told me. "Deep inside you, when all is said and done, when everything is on the line. You know. You fight."

I couldn't find words to say. Nothing quite made sense, not even my confusion. I sat in numb, aching, wondering silence until Pele rumbled again.

"Picking up rocks to stop fires," she mused. "I haven't yet seen a defendant on trial try *that* in the middle of battle. It is

119

more than I expected."

"You *are* more," my mother added in a whisper. "That is why you are the best, Daisy, because you are more than just a guardian. For the rest of us, it was simply a set of rules. You make it more."

Picking up rocks to stop fires. Queen of the garden. In my confused mind, the quotes combined, and almost made me cry for real this time. I felt exactly like Silver-tree stumbling upon a magic fire and asking it foolish questions. *Oh Midsummer flame, who is the best guardian? What should I look like?*

"Maybe that's why I feel like I don't fit," I realized aloud. Like a root between rocks, like the water over the edge of the mountain, I could feel myself spilling over the confines of *guardian.*

Pele stretched blood red wings, her basalt scales cracking and sizzling. "Make something new, then, child. Let yourself grow. The Circle will support you."

Mother glanced at her companion, smiling. "Pele is one of the toughest dragons on the Circle, if not anywhere. You can bet they'll do as she says."

"And they will trust your observations," Pele returned warmly. "Just as they will accept your daughter's."

"I never needed your permission." I said it softly, not not to them but to myself, as I remembered what Rhys had said. *The only authority on the matter is yours.* And what Hunter had said: *sometimes visions are unnecessary. Don't you think?*

"Of course you didn't," my mother agreed.

Pele's tail sparked as she whipped it lazily behind her. "Seems to me that you needed, little one, was a reminder of your limits."

This time I *did* laugh. Because she was exactly right.

Twenty-Two

Delivery Man

Rhys

In the past I might have considered myself a patient man, but I find that did not hold true in this case. Despite my promise to Glacial that I would only act *when it is time,* I found myself itching to go up the mountain the very next morning. All had been quiet, as far as anyone in town could tell, and the wondering was slowly killing me.

Fortunately, Glacial proved better at reading me than I might have expected.

When I showed up at the Pomegranate at opening time, she already had a basket prepared for me; it was full, she assured me, of hearty pies and scones and even a specially-made braided bread. I hardly stayed in place long enough to hear them all described. Without another thought, Nessie and I were headed up to the grotto.

The forest was peaceful, and when I arrived, the garden was almost silent. This worried me for an instant—but quickly I spied a few pixies playing amid the ferns, and I knew matters couldn't be *too* dire.

Still . . . I *was* struck by a heavy sense of intruding.

After a brief vacillation, I gave my basket to the pixies; or, rather, I placed it on the ground near the waterfall, as a few pixies alone could not lift such an object. "This is for Daisy," I told them, slowly and clearly, for pixies have a tendency to listen to only half a sentence.

"Come in, come in, come in!" they chimed.

"I—I will not, today," I said with some reluctance. "I am not expected. I will come tomorrow, and I will bring more food. I will come every day. She can see me when she likes. Will you tell her that?"

"Yes," they all promised, most assiduously.

"And—tell her—that if she does not want me to come, she can let me know by note tomorrow."

"Yes, yes," they promised again, leaving me alone with my doubts.

Well, doubts or no, I was determined to be as good as my word. I came the next day at the same time, this time with a selection of fruits and vegetables along with savory pies; and, to my intense relief, I found no note asking me to cease. Instead there was a swarm of familiar pixies eager to tell me about the dragons' trial.

However, Miss Daisy herself did not appear.

The pixies assured me that at least she was recovering, if not entirely well. They were unclear upon this point themselves;

as a general rule, I have found most pixies to be extraordinarily ignorant of matters such as bodily injury. Deep down I think they are terrified of any kind of injury, and this is why they cling to Daisy so. But I had to admit I was worried. As companions, pixies can be delightful, but as nursemaids they are decidedly lacking.

And I couldn't help but wonder: if Miss Daisy didn't mind me coming, why then would she not see me?

Was she too injured?

On the third day, I put this question to Sha, one of the oldest and most practical pixies. My visits had not yet lost their novelty and we were surrounded by other pixies attempting to peer into the basket (this one held cookies, butter and cream, and fresh banana nut bread) or nestle into Nessie's mane (an occupation which was very much unappreciated by my long-suffering steed).

"She's well enough to walk," the pixie informed me, holding remarkably still amid the chaos. "That's not the reason she doesn't come."

I was a little flustered, and still worried, and I admit I lost a little of my self-control. "Could you tell me what is?"

"I could," came the characteristically capricious answer. "She told me herself this morning."

Normally I wouldn't have pried, but seeing as the conversation had gone this far . . . "What did she say?"

"I haven't figured it out yet," said the pixie, lowering its voice to sound something like Daisy. "I just don't know what to say, and of course the meadowsweet isn't ready. And I am so ashamed about it all, still. I know it is silly, but with the state I'm in, I'm a little afraid to go out."

Afraid? The word went straight through me, reminding me

of unpleasant hints from Sakura as well. This was absolutely not tenable. My lady could be anything she wished, but never afraid of me.

"Take me to see her," I demanded. I didn't like to simply barge in myself, but I *was* unshakably set on straightening this mess out. I am fortunate that the pixies have accepted and trusted me from the beginning, and did not think to take offense at my tone.

The hurricane of glittering wings swept under the waterfall and into the cave, bringing myself along with it. The pixies' cave is a grand and undoubtedly magical place, with glowing, arching ceilings and a magnificent Tree of Life—a sight to truly take one's breath away. I am not certain I was breathing, however. I did not look around, nor even slow down, as I descended into the series of mossy tunnels beneath the Tree where Daisy keeps her own space. I did not notice that fewer and fewer pixies followed. They do not mind exploring, but I think in retrospect they could not keep up with my pace. By the time I got to the little cavern in the back that served as Daisy's kitchen, I think I might have been running. But that lack of decorum, too, I failed to notice.

I did however notice that, when I finally came face to face with her, we were alone.

She was sitting beside her open hearth, though she rose as I approached. A small, controlled fire and simmering pot indicated that she'd been making tea. Perfectly normal . . . And yet, to see her face, illuminated by so many twinkling lights strung along the ceiling, did not feel normal at all.

"The pixies told me you did not want to see me because you were afraid," I said, all in a rush, dropping down to one knee before the fire. "Please don't be afraid. You must know I could not mean you any harm. I was only worried about you. I could never, ever, think any less of you, no matter what happened, no matter if you'd undecided about me or not—"

"But that isn't what I meant. Did they tell you that too?" she interrupted, moving to sit on the stone bench nearest me. "That I was uncertain about you?"

"They—they said you hadn't figured it out."

"Hmm. I think they only told you half of things. Which we might have expected," she said, tilting her lovely head with a rueful smile. "I suppose we should have known better than to try exchanging notes or messages."

"Then—did you mean to leave me a note? Did you wish for me not to come?"

"No, I didn't mean that, either." She shifted to face me directly, laying one hand on my arm. Her other arm, I noticed, was wrapped up in a crude sling. But she gave me no time to stew over this, going on, "My mother and Pele, the dragons who oversaw my trial—they said some things that I was trying to think over, that is all. I wasn't rethinking anything about *you.* Well, except for the way I sent you off . . . I owe you so many apologies, for everything."

My heart was singing now, and I did my best to listen carefully as she went on, "I have been very turned around, thinking I had to be and do *everything,* that it was best that way, or even that it was my job. But Pele and my mother—they reminded me that it is not. Very emphatically," Daisy said with a little weary smile that made my chest ache. "But I was never afraid of *you.* Maybe—definitely—ashamed of how stubborn I have been. But when I told the pixies I was scared, I meant just that I was scared to—to leave the Tree, or to try to make it to Belville. Somehow I must fulfill my promise to Sakura, but I

125

don't know how—we never really did talk about it, and I think I never even told her about the trial . . . At first I thought I would try to take down the meadowsweet myself, but once I'd come in here and hidden myself away . . . it was more difficult than I expected to leave."

There was so much I wanted to say, but I had to be certain of her well being first and foremost. "Your arm?"

"A familiar sight, maybe?" She referred of course to our first encounter with the ice dragon, when she'd injured her wing. My fear seemed justified when she glanced down, biting her lip. "It's—it's much worse this time. I suppose I never did learn my lesson, I just let instinct take over instead of thinking things through. I—I can't fly. Mother said I shouldn't even transform, not until autumn, and that if it weren't for the Tree . . ."

She could have died. Every single thought, every question I'd wanted to ask her, every thing I'd wanted to say, every word I'd ever known flew out of my head.

"Well, anyway," she continued, blushing faintly, "We'd better focus on more practical things. I suppose you know that Saki wanted meadowsweet from our—from the pixies' garden for her Midsummer party tomorrow. Like I said I—I guess I promised her I'd bring it, but—"

The distress in her voice shook me out of my shock. "I will collect it, my lady. I will gather it myself as well. Anything to help."

"Oh—really? You don't mind?" Daisy smiled at me, shyly. "It's supposed to be freshly picked, so we'll have to do it all tomorrow afternoon. I will—I will help, don't worry."

Don't worry! Well, I tried to remind myself, *the worst has passed.* But even then, I could not quite see beyond my fear. "My lady," I managed gruffly, "it would be my honor to act as courier for you."

Twenty-Three

A Pixies' Playdate

Daisy

If this was a proper story, I think, I would have just told Rhys *everything* in that moment when he came in to meet me in the cave. Somehow we would have spilled out everything in our hearts, and—

Well, that's assuming he had things in his heart like I had in mine. That is to say, I did *wonder* if I ought to tell him more—if I ought to say that I'd made a mistake, sending him away—but he didn't seem like he was waiting to hear that. He was very quiet and almost distracted, like he wasn't quite paying attention. Maybe Mother was right, saying that I am proud . . . All I know is I couldn't sit there confessing my love to someone who seemed like they'd rather be somewhere else.

In any case, Rhys left quite quickly, but of course he was as good as his word the next day. The pixies were all abuzz the moment he showed up, right before lunch. I hesitated going to meet him—it really *was* hard to leave the cave, even to go to the garden, after I'd gotten used to hiding again. And he was earlier than I expected. But if I hadn't walked out there myself, I think Goldy and Bree would have dragged me. They get away with so much more pushiness when I am in human form!

As I emerged into the bright light at the center of the garden, leaving the safety of the cave and waterfall behind, the first thing I noticed was the rainbow-colored swarm of pixies all around Rhys and his horse, Nessie. They were so joyful—they do love the summer solstice, and they love Rhys, too. Seeing them fly around him made me remember how I had felt when I first met him. I'd been worried and confused then, too, of course, but there was also that pure delight of stumbling across something *right* . . .

. . . Or perhaps it would be better to say, something that *fit*.

When his blue eyes met mine, I smiled. And then I caught the scent of wholegrain bread and cheese and basil in the air, and I realized why he'd come so early.

"Glacial and Sakura send their regards," he said, as my gaze drifted down to the basket he held in one hand. "And Madame Lavender as well. They are the ones who have been making food for me to bring."

"I did wonder," I admitted, though actually what I wondered about was the fact that he called them *Glacial* and *Sakura*. I'd never noticed he was so friendly with the people at the Pomegranate Café.

Rhys must have sensed the question in my voice—he has often been uncanny that way. "I think you would like Glacial," he added. "She's been very invested in your healing process. That's not to say she's been presumptuous—it's my fault, really, for telling her things—what I meant to say is, I believe she's seen trials of her own."

"It's alright," I told him, because just like he could sense my question before, I could sense his guilty conscience. "I'm sure the whole town wanted to know why there were so many dragons on the mountain all of a sudden. I should have thought of that at the time, but I was very—distracted. But I am very grateful to Glacial, really, and to all of them. It has been . . ."

I let my voice trail off as I gestured vaguely to my arm, tied up in a sling. I didn't wish to complain. And while the pain was always there in my shoulder, it was the exhaustion that had been truly difficult anyway.

Exhaustion from stopping forest fires. I could practically hear Pele's disbelieving, derisive voice in my head. Rather than make me feel ashamed, though, it made me smile faintly.

"Of course it has been difficult," Rhys concluded. He immediately went into that brisk mood of his, something I had seen before. I didn't think it was something he'd learned from being a knight.

Smoothly and quickly, as though he'd done all of this before, he strode to the boulder we often used as a bench and unfurled a checkered blanket over it. The wave of air made the cloud of pixies squeal with glee, and as they surfed the currents, Rhys began unpacking a picnic lunch fit for royalty, laying out bread and butter and cheeses and early summer tomatoes, and utensils and china and even a pitcher of tea. Then he crossed to Nessie (who stood watching this placidly, far too well-mannered to even think of eating the flowers that reached his knees) and took out, of all things, a large purple umbrella.

This he set up so it shaded the boulder, casting tinted light across the crystal glasses and further delighting the pixies, who swarmed it and began sliding down its curved canvas. Finally he looked back at me.

This had taken about two seconds. I'm pretty sure my mouth was open, but no sound came out. In an instant I realized two things: first, that Rhys's "brisk" mode was something he did because he was trying to care for someone, and second, if I didn't climb up and sit on that boulder, he would probably pick me up and set me there himself.

I closed my mouth and crawled up on to the picnic blanket. It wasn't very graceful—it's hard to do anything gracefully when you've got pixies diving off an umbrella over your head and one arm in a sling—but it worked. When I saw how Rhys smiled as he took a seat next to me, my heart melted. *How did I forget that?* I wondered, mesmerized. *When did I forget how much he enjoys showing kindness to his friends?*

We ate quietly for a moment, listening to the pixies and the waterfall and the breeze rustling fragrant leaves all around us. The boulder was like a little island amid rows and rows of flowers.

Eventually, Rhys cleared his throat. "I was remiss, and did not hear the end of your story yesterday," he said quietly. "Do you intend to continue as guardian?"

"For the pixies? Oh, of course," I answered at first. Then I hesitated. "Not that I think they need one any more, strictly speaking. I suppose—well—that is part of what I have been trying to figure out. My problem was I was just too busy thinking about what a guardian should be, what my life *should* look like. Mother and Pele—they were telling me that perhaps I ought to make the role of guardian *more,* that is, more suited to myself, I think. I could change it. And for a while I've been thinking the pixies really don't need me, not in the old way, and they do have you also as guide, so . . ."

I was wondering if he *wanted* to act as their guide, but I was too timid to ask it. And he was thinking of other things, apparently. Without looking up from slicing fresh fruit, he asked, "What would *you* like?"

I sighed. "I'd like to stay. I'll keep being their guardian. I just won't be *only* a guardian. Part-time guardian, maybe? Does that make sense? It's funny how much easier to say it is when speaking to you. In my head I've been so confused about it."

"The phrase you'd like, perhaps, is 'on call,'" he suggested, handing me a little saucer of fresh strawberries. "And if that is the case, and therefore there is a chance you again be exposed to battle, I must—I need to—I would be *very* gratified if I could teach you some things about self-defense."

"You would?" I blinked. *So maybe he does want to stay on?*

"I am not saying that you need always fight. And naturally, I respect that most of your duties as guardian, you've been able to resolve peacefully." *And by that,* I thought, smiling, *he means, 'just the sight of you was intimidating enough.'* He went on, "But given your repeated history, it might be wise to—channel the power that you have. Of course I can not teach you anything about aerial tactics, but I am certain there are some principles that will be useful to you, and if—if it will prevent you from relying on strategies that involve *landing yourself on the battlefield underneath a larger opponent*—"

Even in the shade of the umbrella, I flushed. "How did you know that's what I did?"

"Call it experience." He didn't say anything more, just pressed his lips into a very firm line, like the whipped cream he was doling out had done something inexcusable.

For some reason, the sight made me chuckle. He met my eyes quickly, surprised, and the effect just made me more amused. For the first time all summer, I leaned my head back and really laughed.

When I'd collected myself I almost apologized—until I saw that he was grinning, too, as he watched me. So instead I said, "You got all that just from seeing my arm like this, didn't you? You sound just like Mother and Pele. I think you're right, you know. I'd be very glad if you would help me practice something better. Not that I necessarily want to fight again either, but one thing I've learned is you never *do* know what will happen . . . And neither myself nor the pixies are as good a healer as you."

"Me, a healer?" He caught his breath, like he was taken aback. Part of me worried I'd said something wrong, somehow. But then he looked around at the garden, almost like he was seeing it for the first time.

"You have almost everything you need here already," he said cryptically.

"Of course. You helped us start most of it." My voice faltered, and I added, "But that doesn't mean we know what to do with it. The herbs and things, I mean. And—it would be good to put it to use."

"Yes, I suppose that is true . . ." he turned back to me, and that speculative look faded as he smiled. "For this afternoon, let's focus on the meadowsweet, shall we?"

Twenty-Four

Queen of the Meadow

Rhys

My lady's garden is well cared for, and would indeed make an excellent resource for an aspiring healer. But it is not, admittedly, particularly organized. The ridge creates a V shape, running from the waterfall at its point out to deep forest; in the sunlight that fills the center of the triangle, flowers of every shape and size abounded. As Daisy had said, I *had* helped her and the pixies clear the space and begin the garden, but even in my previous visits I had been too preoccupied to notice how lush it had become. *Soon,* I couldn't help but think, *we will need to clear back some more of the undergrowth, and give it more space; and perhaps add paths and trellises . . .*

But of course, I hadn't *actually* secured any right to thinking about the future that way. My lady had agreed to martial training, which made me almost giddy with relief, but we hadn't yet broached more serious matters. And standing hip deep in wildflowers trying to keep up while Daisy instructed the pixies where to cut and I caught the stalks in a growing bundle didn't seem the place to bring up things like *I've been such a fool* or *did you really mean it when you said we should separate? Because a certain shadow witch says you didn't* . . .

I will admit to *one* service Sakura did for me—just the one, though there may be more. By demanding meadowsweet in particular, she'd piqued the pixies' curiosity. The more we harvested, the more determined they were to *see* this party at the Pomegranate. And once the pixies decided they wanted to go, it was child's play to convince my lady to make an appearance as well.

"We'll just go for a little while," she told them, looking both stricken and half tempted, in that way which only Daisy can. "We don't have to stay the whole time, especially once people start showing up. I'm not even getting dressed up. And the moment you all get tired, or anything happens, I want you all to come back here as fast as you can—do you hear me? I won't be able to fly with you, so you have to look after yourselves!"

I will look after you, I thought. But in that moment Nessie, loaded down with flowers, knelt beside my lady so that she could climb up into his saddle. Apparently, it was already time to leave.

It was hours later when I next had a moment to myself to think. Predictably, "a little while" had come to mean "past sunset." The pixies adored the tea shop, promptly infesting its every nook and cranny the moment we'd arrived. Daisy then offered to help Sakura and Emmelayne set out the meadowsweet centerpieces as a way to "make up" for nearly missing her delivery, and shortly afterward Sakura had declared that my attempts to help were "getting in the way." I was put on bonfire duty, exiled to a convenient bit of Market Square in front of the café. As soon as I had the wood lit, townsfolk began arriving. It was twilight before Officer Thorn decided to take over fire duties from me.

Grateful, but also perhaps a bit peeved, I made my way into the café in search of refreshment—and Daisy. Instead a most unwelcome stranger stood behind the counter.

"Ah, if it isn't Rhys, at last," he said, rather smugly. He wore a Pomegranate Café apron and seemed to have assumed Sakura's duties—he certainly held himself as though he were ruling over the solstice party. Which, I had to admit, wasn't entirely inappropriate—given that we were celebrating a holiday of wild and natural abundance.

Unaffected by my scowl, he continued, "Loosen up, my friend. Look at the magic you have brought here."

He gestured at the busy café around us: excited townsfolk clustered around tables, burning meadowsweet over candles and chattering about what they'd seen in the flames; the local Witch in the corner plying a lighthearted tune on a stringed instrument of some variety; pixies flittering through the air, popping out of knickknacks, scattering flower petals from the balcony. The light from their little wings alone was enough to give the café a glow, despite the growing darkness outside.

"It is Miss Daisy's doing," I informed the person behind the counter.

"And who brought Miss Daisy here?" he returned. "The two of you have done well with your gifts. In fact, I might go so far as to say I find it *inspiring*."

I studied him carefully, any idea of reverence or caution forgotten. Though he'd parroted my respectful title for Daisy, he didn't seem to be making fun of me. He actually seemed to be having genuine fun.

"Where is she now?" I asked, a little less coolly, but still determined not to be drawn into his game of cryptic references.

"Right here, Rhys," my lady answered. She appeared out of the crowd beside me, hair a little mussed and shoulders drooping a little with fatigue, but beaming the most beautiful smile I'd ever seen. I think my knees might have buckled had I not been immediately steadied by two more unexpected appearances.

"We were testing out the meadowsweet divination, finding out who our true loves will be," said Sakura, at Daisy's elbow. Then, seeing the look on my face, she added, "We've actually just been talking about cleaning up the backyard and adding a patio and garden. Calm down, won't you?"

"We could have a fire back there next year. Instead of in the Square," Glacial added more quietly, lingering in Daisy's shadow.

"Why not have both?" asked the person behind the counter, jovial. "The more the merrier."

Glacial met his gaze, and for a moment I saw in her face the exact same thing I felt in my heart: a wariness yet almost a willingness, something poets far better than me have likened to that first moment after a bird launches itself into the air, when it is falling just before its wings have caught the breeze.

"I have to warm up another batch of honey cakes," she said abruptly. With a flash of a white tail, she was gone.

"She's got a point. At the moment, we have plenty of customers already, just with *one* bonfire," Sakura said. In that moment my heart swelled. It seemed to me that the shadow witch *was* a good friend, and that the wounded baker would find her strength in time.

"Next year, you might find you're ready to take the next step," the stranger said vaguely, nose pointed toward the kitchens.

"Yes, well, some of us have the *present* to think about." Sakura glanced between Daisy and myself, one eyebrow arched. "Since the pixies seem to be enjoying themselves, I take it you both are staying a while? Why don't you grab some food and find a quiet place to catch your breath? I think the table in the corner of the front patio just opened up."

Convenient. I was almost nervous as my lady and I gathered drinks and plates piled high with grilled foods and, of course, cupcakes before making our way outside.

Night had fallen, but the Square in front of the Pomegranate was just as alive as the inside of the café. Fireflies and stray pixies lit up the park, dancing around the bonfire, which had grown considerably under Officer Thorn's supervision. Across the corner, I caught a glimpse of Red, Luca, and William sitting on her shop's front steps. Other groups loitered in the street and dotted the grass, talking and laughing amongst themselves.

"It seems like the party's going really well," Daisy said, a little breathless as we sat side by side, looking out over the park. As she set her belated dinner on the table in front of us, she added, "I'm glad we came."

"As am I," I said, hesitantly laying meaning into the words.

She caught my intention and looked up, smiling. "You know, I was thinking about what Saki said, just now, about the meadowsweet. It made me remember something Goldy told me."

"It did?" I asked, promptly dropping a skewer of roasted red peppers.

"Queen of the garden," Daisy said, oblivious to my distress. "She called me that, back before the trial. I thought she was making fun of me. Then, later, it actually made me feel—well, silly. But I think I get it now. She wanted me to relax and to see what I *am,* instead of what I would be in the future, or what I thought I should be."

"That also sounds like something Sakura would say," I ventured cautiously.

"Doesn't it? And yet Saki says she can't follow the pixies at all when they talk," Daisy chuckled.

For a moment we sat in companionable silence. As grateful as I was, though, my heart was racing. I wondered if now, at last, I ought to say something . . .

But my lady beat me to it. "Actually, thinking about it all now, there's a lot of things I still haven't had a chance to say, Rhys," she said slowly. "I know the whole point of the solstice is how fleeting time is, how we have to appreciate these moments when they're here, and yet . . ."

"Please," I said softly, "say whatever you like."

Daisy ran her hands through her mussed hair before turning back to me, head tilted, her smile rueful. "I said yesterday I owed you an apology, but I guess I never fully gave it. The truth is, I was wrong to end things with you so abruptly. I was so confused and worried over the pixies' new life, and mine, and—and *ours.* And I let that confusion reflect on you, pushing you away even if maybe—maybe you wanted to stay." She glanced at me, trepidation clear in her face. "I was wondering . . . If I *was* to play Saki's party game, and look in the flames to see my true love . . . Well, I think it would look like you. I think maybe I don't need to look, because I already know."

"Not quite," I said, with excruciating difficulty.

139

Surprise flickered over her. "What do you mean?"

"That I have erred, my lady, in not showing you all of me. I left you in doubt as to what I wanted; I said so many things, but not the most important. As a result, your image of me might not include the most vital parts."

"So . . . what didn't you show?" she asked, her voice no more than a breath.

"That I am not a knight. I am not anything, except a shopkeeper's assistant, now, and apparently—apparently, a friend. Perhaps a healer. And—despite anything else, the things I thought I was or might be or never realized, I am and have always been in love with you."

Her eyes were iridescent. "Rhys. Is that—is that enough? Is that all you want to be?"

"Daisy," I said finally, "to be all those things honestly, truly, takes everything I have. They are the best I can be. If you *could* see me in the midsummer fires, what I am and will be, then I would be glad if that is what you saw."

She leaned from her chair and wrapped her good arm around my neck, but not before I saw the tears glistening in her eyes. "Oh, my love. I'm so glad you said something! This is what I have been trying to figure out, all this time. You put it perfectly."

"Then—you do not mind, if I am not exactly as you thought?"

"Mind?" She pulled back far enough to look at me, and then beamed her delight. "Did I forget to say it, again? Oh, I've been so afraid to. I've been so caught up in trying to be stronger and trying so hard not to waste time, like I had to prove myself, exactly like you said. I've been looking at things backwards, from the outside in. But it is *better* this way, where it's not about what we expect to see, but what is actually there. *Inside*, in my heart, all along, you've been there. You're right in saying the best we can be is honest, Rhys. And I love you, too, so very much."

As if to prove this, she pressed herself into me again, this time kissing me with a warmth and passion which was, quite honestly, nothing short of magical.

"I had intended to listen," I murmured when we stopped to breathe, still a little dazed by the suddenness of her in my arms. "All this time, trying to make amends. I wasn't sure how. I hadn't intended to dictate the conversation . . ."

"Rhys, sweet one," Daisy laughed, "Don't you worry. I think we both have plenty of listening yet to do."

Epilogue

Sakura

It's not every day you see a knight and dragon learn that being strong actually means being vulnerable, is it?

That is, of course, as long as we're not talking leaving-your-weak-spots-unguarded-in-an-actual-fight vulnerable.

But what do I know about battles? Certainly far less than Daisy, for all her protests. In fact, all I can be relied upon to know is tea and parties, and I'm learning more about those all the time. And good thing, too, because the people of Belville seem more and more interested in them. Litha went so well that we decided to host a series of smaller parties throughout the summer. Of course, we couldn't host Hunter and a bunch of pixies at every single one, but we still managed to have fun.

It was, in fact, at another summer bonfire that I next saw Daisy and Rhys. I think I might not have seen them at all if I hadn't taken the liberty of sending Daisy an invitation. After the big hit her pixies had been at the solstice, it seemed only fair to invite her to a party where she didn't have to feel responsible for the main attraction. This bonfire was a much smaller affair—just a neighborhood gathering, really. But I figured that would be more her speed. (Plus, I was curious about an update. Wouldn't you be?)

And by *her*, I mean *them*, naturally, for Rhys would be the one to give Daisy a ride into town on that ridiculous magical horse of his.

I found Rhys and Daisy tucked around a little table on the café's patio. It was a nice little spot, shaded, and removed from the noise of the Square while still having a view of the twilight gathering. Despite the fact that the Pomegranate's patio chairs are distinctly one-person-only—I should know, I picked them out when I decorated—the lovebirds were sitting close as could be, and Rhys had his arm around Daisy's shoulder as firelight danced across their faces.

"So," I said, dropping into a free chair near their table, "what do you think of our party? Not as good as Litha, maybe, but not so bad?"

"Not so bad," Daisy agreed, smiling at me. "The iced tea is lovely, and I liked the lemon cupcakes. The pixies will be glad to hear about it."

"I'll give you the extras, if we have any, and you can take them home with you," I promised before grinning particularly at Rhys. "What? I'm not interrupting anything, am I?"

"Miss Sakura," the ex-knight returned. He was cool, but not as prickly as he might once have been. "One wonders if you are ever *not* interrupting something."

"I thought we agreed, no more formality. We're all friends here." I grinned at Daisy this time, and she chuckled. I wondered if she knew exactly how prickly her knight had

143

been in her absence! But there was no need to bring it up. "Besides, everyone's left the café for the moment, and I distinctly remember purchasing this chair, so that must mean it's mine. You wouldn't expect someone with two fake feet to stand *all* night, would you?"

"You do very well," Daisy said, and then blushed. "I don't mean that in any patronizing way. Only—"

Naturally I had noticed how her left arm was still carefully tucked in a sling over her floral dress. When her gaze trailed down, I told her, "It does take getting used to, any kind of injury, even if it's only temporary."

"You will recover," Rhys added to her very gently. "Particularly if you let it be."

Daisy made a charmingly childlike face of impatience and frustration at me before smiling and laughing at herself. "Rhys has taken over all first aid at the Tree, and that's probably for the best."

"Daisy already has the start of an exemplary medicinal garden in the grotto," Rhys added, not to be outdone.

"Maybe that's something else we can contribute to the town, if it does well," she agreed, turning back to me with her eyes alight. "I know Hunter brings your tea, but you or Red or whoever wants the herbs could have them, if we have extra. And I think we will—the pixies have really taken to caring for them."

"We will pay you for them," I told her firmly, because I could already see that this might be the start of a bright future—provided one or both of them treated it with a little practical sense. And no doubt having a little medicinal competition around town would do Trent some good. "Let Hunter stick to his own business. He told me to give you his regards, by the way, and to congratulate you on the outcome of your trial. I'm afraid he's had to leave town—he often comes and goes like that."

Rhys said nothing, but he smiled faintly at me, which spoke volumes. Daisy reached out to brush my hand and said, "Thank you for the message, and for your support. And—I think we have many other things to thank you for, too. It seems to me . . . I might still be alone, up at the Tree, in pain and trying to teach the pixies how to make a sling, if you and the others hadn't encouraged Rhys to say something. And to come all the way up to the Tree with such good food."

"I spoke entirely on my own," he protested.

"Of course you did," Daisy answered sweetly. "But would you have felt you *could* say something, left to your own devices? Besides, the food did give you a perfect opportunity. And then the party, of course."

It was the perfect answer. I had to hand it to her—she knew exactly how to deal with her knight, and I was impressed. Wonders continued when Rhys not only acquiesced, but turned to me and admitted,

"I would doubtless have remained down here, alone, for much longer . . . had I not been strengthened by the support of friends."

"Well, then, you're *both* welcome for the support, and for the party," I decided, satisfied. One more satisfied matchmaking customer, and a new source of herbs, too! "And since it's still sort of Midsummer, I'll add, *thank you* to you both for trusting me. Eventually."

Daisy must have intuited that that last word was meant for Rhys, because she let it slide. Instead, looking out into the twilight, she mused, "Yes—a time of abundance and gratitude, even when things don't go to plan. It is very fitting, I think.

But, Saki . . . what about our friend, Glacial?"

So they weren't so wrapped up in their own problems that they didn't notice, I thought, grinning a little, just to myself. Glacial was hiding in her kitchen by now, so I didn't have to worry about her seeing my plotting. Was it my fault if her cleaning kept her from hearing all the gossip—particularly the gossip about herself? "Oh, don't worry about Glacial. She just needs a little time."

And maybe, I decided, as we sipped our iced teas, *another little helping hand.*

About the Author

Elle adores happy endings, fairy tales, and above all, learning new things. As a historian and educator, she believes in the value of stories as a mirror for complicated realities. She currently lives in New Jersey with a grumpy tortoise and a three-legged cat.

Find more stories set in Belville at ellehartford.com. And while you're there, sign up for Elle's newsletter to get bonus material like a map of the Pomegranate, free short stories, and extra epilogues!

And *stay tuned!* More stories from the Pomegranate will be on their way soon. In the meantime, if you loved this one, Elle and Sakura will be eternally grateful if you left a review!

Also by Elle Hartford

If you enjoyed your time at the Pomegranate, consider checking out the first novella, *Worthy in Love*! And the story of Daisy and Rhys' encounter with the ice dragon can be found in *A Tale of Rowan and Daisy,* available to newsletter subscribers or in print.

Worthy in Love
Valentine's Day has come to Belville, and with it, a grand opening auction at the Pomegranate Café. Can Ryuko and Mel, opposites and enemies at first sight, come together to make the holiday event truly magical? Or will shadows of the past overtake them?

https://books2read.com/worthy-in-love